A Ride to Freedom

OLIVIA TUFFIN

nosy
crow

PROLOGUE

The woman had pale hair the colour of wheat and cornflower-blue eyes. Her eyes sparkled as she watched the dark-haired boy canter a circle on his pony, the sweetest grey Welsh mountain mare with a pink snip between her nostrils. The boy wore a look of grim determination as he clung to the pony's white mane. Despite his small stature, the boy showed an incredible strength as he pulled himself up to a standing position, arms stretched to the sides, the determined look now replaced by one of pure joy as he circled the meadow, laughing out loud.

"Wonderful!" the woman called, her voice soft and full of love, a voice that gave no trace of fear of the trials that lay ahead – the endless hospital visits, the treatments. Or sadness as she thought of the hushed voice of the doctor as he told her the prognosis.

They practised every afternoon after school, precious hours lost in the wildflower meadows, just the two of them and their ponies. For the boy, who struggled with everyday life, who found school both frustrating and bewildering, who was happiest with the horses, it was the best part of the day.

"That'll do. Easy now." The woman's voice slowed the pony who lowered her head as the boy

climbed down from his standing position. The pony then approached the woman and placed an adoring muzzle against her arm, responding to her praise.

The woman smiled broadly. "Finn, you're getting better every day!" Then she paused and looked towards the horizon. "I hope you'll always carry on stunt riding."

And the boy nodded earnestly, curling his arms round his grey pony.

"Always," he promised her. "Always for you, Mum."

Chapter 1

"OK, Mum, just a few more bits to find. Passport, vetting certificate, travel documents … and I think that's it!" Thirteen-year-old Alice Smalley carefully consulted the list she was holding while her mum rifled through the filing cabinets.

"There we are." Josephine, Alice's mum, pulled out a stack of paperwork, before smiling at her. "Your first trip abroad! And with Secret! Are you

sure you'll be OK?"

"We'll be fine, Mum," Alice replied, ignoring her nerves. She'd never gone away on her own before. She'd never taken part in school trips, even the one to the Lake District where everyone had got soaked! It had been the talk of the school, but Alice had missed out – the ponies and her mum's showing yard taking priority. But this was different. Alice was going away with her beloved roan pony Secret, and not just down the road; she and Secret were setting sail and travelling across the English Channel to France!

It still hadn't sunk in that Alice was going. The trip had come about so fast, and with a break in the showing schedule and the summer holidays underway her mum had agreed. The trip was a visit to a beautiful riding stables with other pony club members from all over the country, to take part in the *Festival du Cheval* – Festival of the Horse.

On the final day of the festival the pony club members were going to participate in a prestigious showjumping competition against contestants from French clubs. But they'd be able to enjoy the rest of the festival during their stay, with lessons and hacking on the agenda.

When June Darby, the district commissioner of Hilltops pony club, had announced back in March that three members of the branch would be selected at random to go on the trip, Alice had put her name down, not expecting much. But Alice and Secret had been drawn from the hat, along with a boy called Sam and a girl called Holly.

Alice had been very relieved that Hannah wasn't coming on the trip. Hannah, the most popular girl in the pony club, had caused a huge amount of heartache over the winter, coming between Alice and her friend Finn. And on the night of Hannah's fourteenth birthday party Alice's mum's beloved

Highland pony, Lachlan, had been killed in an accident, thanks to the actions of Hannah's friends. The teenagers had accidentally let Ella, a pony Finn had rescued from Spain, escape into a terrible snow storm. During her rescue Lachlan had been hit by a speeding car. He'd suffered catastrophic injuries to his leg and had to be put to sleep.

A whinny from the stable yard brought Alice back to the present, and she smiled. Such an insistent call could only belong to Secret. If he knew Alice was nearby, he would whinny and bang on the door until she came and said hello. Slipping out of the door, Alice crossed the yard, pausing as she always did next to Lachlan's stable, which had been left empty. Her mum had folded his navy Olympia rug over the manger, and Fergus, the head groom, had fitted Lachlan's horseshoes to the door in tribute. As always, a lump formed in Alice's throat as she brushed the horseshoes with her fingertips.

She missed the gentle Highland dreadfully.

And there was Secret. In the cool of his stable, trailing his hay over the door, there was a cheerful glint in his dark eyes as he rubbed his head against Alice's arm. Haymaking was taking place all over the county, and the sweet scent of cut grass was heavy in the air. Next door to him, Ella, his best friend, popped her head over her door and whickered in greeting.

"Hello, you!" Alice grinned. She gave the grey mare a scratch on the neck, marvelling as she always did at the change in the pony. She was plump from Alice's mum's excellent grazing, her coat soft and shiny, her ears forward. It was such a change from the defensive, angry pony who had arrived at the start of the year. Finn and his dad, who together had rescued the mare from Spain, had signed her over to Josephine after she and Ella had formed a strong bond.

Since Lachlan's death, Alice had noticed that her mum was somehow softer. She enjoyed spending time with Ella and had even scaled back her showing, taking in a few youngsters, but encouraging Alice more with her showjumping. Back in February, Alice had made the pony club showjumping team as a reserve member, allowing her to train with the team without the pressure of the competitions.

Just then, both Secret and Ella looked up and whinnied in unison, and as Alice turned she felt familiar butterflies in her stomach as Finn approached, riding hat swinging off his arm, dark hair tangled, worn cowboy boots scuffing the yard floor.

Finn was never particularly smiley, but even so Alice noticed he looked especially grim today, a deep frown etched on his face. She rolled her eyes. No doubt he'd been arguing with Sasha, his feisty older sister, *again*. Alice knew things got strained at Finn's home, Rookham Manor, especially now his dad had returned from his travels. The siblings were fiercely loyal to each other, but they fell out all the time! Finn and Sasha had a pony display team, the Flying Fillies, which performed locally, and Finn also rode ponies for Josephine.

"What's up?" Alice asked. "Sash again?"

Only yesterday, Finn had been complaining that his older sister had decided to change the music at one of their displays last-minute. Sasha was spontaneous, creative and bursting with a million ideas, and Alice knew it drove Finn mad at times.

There was the smallest of pauses before Finn shook his head, his features softening. For a second he looked completely lost in thought.

Alice gave a little smile. He always looked so much nicer when he wasn't cross.

"Sort of," he said. "Just some stuff at home. You know, the usual."

Alice nodded, though that could mean anything when it came to Finn and his family. Finn normally talked to her about it when they were out riding. They could talk about anything when out on the ponies, as if being in the saddle gave them both extra confidence. Finn had come over today to school Archie, Samantha's beautiful Fell pony. Samantha was a client of Josephine who'd become a good friend of the yard.

"I thought I'd take Archie up to the top field, practise our extensions," Finn said, changing the subject. "Want to come with me?"

Alice grinned. "Yes please!"

"Cool," Finn smiled. Then his eyes sparkled. "Hey, do you need to *unpack* your saddle first?"

"Ha ha!" Alice stuck her tongue out. They weren't going to France for another week, but ultra-organised Alice was already packed, so desperate not to forget anything. Of course, she had to keep unpacking things every time she wanted to ride, which Finn liked to tease her about.

"You're a funny one," he said warmly, and Alice felt a tingle run through her. She often thought about what Finn had said to her as they rode home together in the snow with Secret and Ella during the night of Ella's rescue. Every now and then she would play the words over in her head: *'Turning up to a party in old jods and still looking beautiful, riding to the rescue of a pony in the snow. If I had a type … that would be it.'* But Finn hadn't said anything like that since, despite the fact he and Alice saw each other most days now.

A short time later, Alice and Secret were riding alongside Finn and Archie, winding their way up to the schooling field. Alice examined her pale arms, enjoying the warmth of the sunshine.

"I wonder how hot it will be in France," she said thoughtfully.

"Super-hot," Finn said, turning to her and giving her the full benefit of his smile. "I can't wait! I love the sun."

At first, Alice thought she'd misheard him. Why would Finn be looking forward to France? He wasn't going on the trip! Alice stared at him, perplexed.

"France," Finn repeated, still grinning. "You know that country, just across the sea? Baguettes and croissants, and, um, snails?"

"Snails!" Alice exploded in laughter. "What are you talking about? You're not coming to France?" She looked at him, aware her cheeks were growing pink. "*Are* you?"

Finn nodded. "Yep," he said. "June asked me. Even though I'm not a member there were places for helpers, so she asked if I'd like to go."

"That's amazing!" Alice cried. "Why didn't you tell me before?"

"It just got confirmed this morning," Finn grinned. "It's good, isn't it?"

Alice nodded, still hardly daring to believe it. She knew that June thought the world of Finn and his dad, and Alice couldn't think of anyone better than Finn to help with the ponies. Her, Secret and now Finn off on a fantastic French adventure! She really couldn't wait.

Chapter 2

Alice awoke early on the day of the departure, long before her alarm. Lying still for a moment, listening to the birds and the occasional snort from the ponies, she smiled. Today it was really happening! A week of fun rides, and the festival, and instruction, and the big showjumping competition. Alice *really* wanted to do well and show everyone how far they'd come!

Alice and Secret had got off to a rocky start with the group lessons at pony club, and for a while Alice had wondered if they were ever going to find their way. It had taken until the night of Hannah's party and Ella's escape to make Alice realise that, when it counted, she *could* fully trust Secret. The little roan had led the frightened Spanish pony back home in the dark, and just a few weeks later Alice and Secret had jumped beautifully at the team trials, earning them their reserve spot.

They'd had a brilliant time training with the team and Angus, Finn's dad. A few weeks previously, after one of the team members' ponies had gone lame, Alice had even represented the branch, jumping a perfect clear round and helping the team into third place. It had been a brilliant moment, but it wasn't always easy. Alice still had huge moments of self-doubt, and at times she felt she was going backwards, not fully trusting her

own judgement. She hoped the French trip would be a turning point, for both her and Secret.

★

Pulling on a hoodie and tying her pale hair into a ponytail, Alice sloped into the yard. Grabbing Secret's head collar, she headed out to his paddock. He was standing nose to tail with Ella, red and white together, their coats shiny in the pink tendrils of sunshine that were just starting to creep over the fields. Alice felt her heart swell with love as she approached Secret. It was time to get him ready for the big trip ahead.

Secret, however, had other ideas.

Ears pricked, the little gelding promptly spun round, cantering off in a cloud of dust, Ella close behind, their tails fanned out. Alice rolled her eyes. It was Secret's favourite trick. Even though Alice had always been the only one who could catch Secret, every now and again he would try it on.

"Fine," Alice said in a mock cross voice. "I'll just sit here."

It was the only way she'd get a head collar on Secret. Rattling a feed bucket didn't work any more; he was far too clever. When she'd been at her wits' end Finn had suggested ignoring Secret. Lying back on the damp grass, Alice closed her eyes, letting the early-morning sun wash over her as the haze lifted. Smiling with her eyes still closed she heard the gentle thud of hooves approach, and then squealed as Secret stuck a bristly muzzle right in her face, nibbling at her hair and breathing his sweet pony breath. She opened one eye, grinning up at him as she gently batted him away.

"Got you!"

★

"Are you *sure* you've packed everything?" Josephine was fretting as Alice dragged her suitcase out into the yard later that morning.

She seemed to have packed a lot of clothes for a week, as the itinerary included a party, plus the general festival celebrations. And that was before she'd even thought of her riding kit. As well as her day-to-day riding clothes she also needed her smart competition gear. And her swimming kit, and shorts … then there was Secret's gear, which was already piled up in the yard. So, when Finn came sauntering through the gate carrying a small black holdall, Alice thought again that she might have slightly overpacked!

"Alice, remember the fly repellent and the aftersun, and *please* don't get sunburnt." Alice's mum was unzipping her suitcase again. Finn placed his holdall down and sat on it, grinning.

"M-um!" Alice could feel herself growing hotter. "I've got everything!"

"Not quite, Al!" To Alice's horror, her dad emerged from the house carrying a scruffy toy pig with one eye and faded pink fur. "You forgot Mr Pigs!"

Alice wanted the ground to open up underneath her. Mr Pigs was a childhood toy who still slept on her bed. Truthfully, she hadn't meant to leave him behind, but why did her dad have to bring him out right now?

"Thanks, Dad," she muttered, grabbing the pig and quickly stuffing him inside her suitcase, hardly daring to look at Finn.

"Oh, Alice." Josephine put her arms round her. "I'll miss you, and Secret."

"I'll miss you too, Mum and Dad," Alice said. But although she really *would* miss her parents, and Poppy the dog, and the yard ponies, she was *so* excited about the trip! A minibus was coming to collect her and Finn, and Secret was going to be loaded on to a specialist horse transporter along with the other Hilltops ponies. As the huge silver

lorry eased its way into the yard it even dwarfed Josephine's big black lorry.

Finn whistled through his teeth. "Look at that!" he remarked. "It's bigger than a house."

Alice remembered the first time he'd seen her mum's lorry. That had been where 'Alice in her palace', his nickname for her, had come from, and she'd hated it!

"Perhaps the Fillies will have a lorry like that soon, with all the bookings you've got," she said, turning to smile at Finn.

Was she imagining it, or did Finn's face darken for just a second? Then he smiled. "Yeah. Maybe."

Secret came out of his stable with a spring in his step.

"Hello, boy." The driver gave him a friendly pat. "Ready to go?"

Secret willingly bounded up the ramp, mirroring Alice's excitement. Alice had never travelled separately to the little gelding, but they'd be right behind in the minibus, which had just pulled up into the yard.

There was a rush of goodbyes and Alice hugged her parents before climbing on to the bus after Finn. Only June was on the bus so far, and Alice sat in the seat opposite her, taking a deep breath as they followed the silver lorry down the drive. As her parents became smaller and smaller in the distance, Alice smiled. They were off on their most exciting adventure to date!

★

After they'd picked up the other pony club members, Sam and his pony Wanda, and Holly and her pony Minstrel, they soon reached the ferry terminal, all full of excitement. It felt strange getting on to the ferry without being able to go and check on Secret, but the driver of the lorry was the only one allowed in the hold. It was a perfect day

for sailing, the sea as smooth as a mirror, and there wasn't a cloud in the sky. The teenagers trooped up after June to the passenger area, but as Alice felt the ferry pull away from the terminal and out into the open water she suddenly felt a bit queasy.

Finn turned to look at her. "Alice? You look very pale. Do you get seasick?"

Alice shrugged. "I don't know," she muttered. "I've never been on a ferry."

"Hey, Alice!" Holly bounded over. She had wild blonde curls framing an impish face and was a bundle of energy, always leaping about. Until the previous year she'd captained the Prince Philip Cup team, and Alice knew she'd been brilliant at it.

"Wooooo!" Holly grinned as the ferry pushed forward. "Feel that? We're into deep water now!"

And with that, Alice's tummy gave an almighty lurch, and she clamped a hand to her mouth, thinking she might throw up. *Oh no! Not in front of Finn!* she thought, feeling her back prickle with sweat. She hoped Secret wasn't feeling seasick too.

"Alice? You OK?" Holly said, putting an arm round her. Alice could only move her head slightly from side to side, terrified if she opened her mouth she'd be sick.

Finn smiled sympathetically, pulling a bottle of water from his bag. "Sit down. I'll stay right here with you. You'll be fine."

And after that, as Holly bounded off to take photos, Finn didn't leave Alice's side, distracting her with funny pony stories, and laughing about the time he'd first met Alice and Secret, when Secret had crashed his way through a country fair.

"It made my day that the runaway pony was followed by such a pretty owner ... even if she had sat in muck!" he grinned, and, blushing, Alice found she felt a bit better.

★
★   ★

★

Alice felt well enough to go outside towards the end of the journey and enjoyed the fresh salty air as she and Finn tried to be the first to spot France. As the huge ferry pulled smoothly into the dock, she wondered if Secret knew they had arrived.

While the transporter dealt with all the paperwork, Alice reboarded the minibus. She was soon asleep, able to nap anywhere after years of long journeys in the horsebox with her mum. It felt as though only five minutes had passed before she was being shaken awake by Finn.

Alice sat up in confusion, and then blushed as she realised that she'd fallen asleep on Finn's shoulder and he'd put his arm round her. Her tummy flipped upside down... She hoped she hadn't dribbled on him!

Finn was smiling. "We've arrived at the overnight stop. Good job – my shoulder was getting tired!"

"Where's Secret?" she asked, wide awake now. The minibus was bumping along a dusty track next to a field full of sunflowers, eventually coming to a stop outside a pretty house.

"Just behind us," Finn said. "He'll be glad to stretch his legs."

So am I, Alice thought, slowly unfolding her own long legs and following the others out.

The warm sunshine washed over her, and the air seemed to hum with the sound of crickets. To the left of the house was a huge pony field and to the right was a meadow where tents were all set up. To Alice's relief, the silver lorry then eased its way up the drive and there was a familiar whinny. Secret!

After hugging the little Welsh gelding, Alice turned him out with the other ponies, and they all rolled luxuriously before putting their heads down to graze. Alice and Holly ran around exploring

the meadows, enjoying the last of the evening sunshine. Alice didn't think she could feel happier. It was going to be the best week ever – she was sure of it!

★

Later that evening, after a barbecue, Alice wandered back over to see Secret. As she made her way over to the field the chirrups of the crickets got louder and the meadow grasses brushed her bare legs. Secret trotted over to see her and she smiled. "So proud of you today, boy," she said, running her hand through his mane. Then she frowned, hearing a familiar voice. It was Finn, on his mobile.

"Really?" He sounded shocked.

Alice knew she shouldn't be listening in, but it was impossible not to. She stood quietly, unsure what to do. There was a pause.

"What are we going to do?" Finn was speaking again. "That doesn't give us long, does it? Where

are you going to find a thousand? So that's it..."
Another pause. "I know, Dad, I know. You always
say that, but it's not worth it, is it? It's just not
worth it..."

Chapter 3

Alice made her way quietly back to the group and Finn joined them a minute or so later. Finn didn't say anything when he returned, but he seemed very distracted. Whatever was going on at Rookham Manor sounded serious ... and Alice wondered who wanted £1,000, and what for. But Finn's dad Angus was at home and in charge now, so surely he could sort out whatever problem they were facing? With everyone gathered round the campfire she didn't have a chance to talk to Finn on his own, and he headed to bed early. Frowning, Alice watched him go. She guessed he'd tell her what was going on when he was ready…

★

They had another couple of hours of driving in the morning before they arrived at the equestrian centre. Alice felt a leap of excitement as the minibus pulled off the road. They dipped down a short sharp hill, crossing a trickle of water before lumbering up again and carrying on up a long drive of a mile or more that was flanked by trees

White post-and-rail fencing divided the land either side into dusty paddocks, and each paddock was swarming with activity. The festival was due to start the very next day and there were teams of people everywhere setting up rings full of shiny showjumps, a huge yellow and white circus tent

and even a Ferris wheel! Alice craned her neck to see as much as she could as they passed the big arena. She and Secret would soon be jumping in that ring, she thought excitedly.

"That little dip we drove through is where the ford usually is, but it's dry at the moment. I've been told when it rains it can get rather deep, so let's hope we avoid any storms!" June beamed at the riders and nodded at the huge honey-coloured house in front of them. "And here we are!"

The first thing Alice noticed when she climbed out of the minibus was the smell. The warm air was heavily scented with lavender and beyond the house, which was more like a castle, purple fields stretched into the distance. The second thing Alice noticed was the boy who stood by the gates smiling broadly. He was about her age, maybe slightly older, and had the tousled blond, tanned look of a surfer, only he was dressed in a blue striped

★
★
31
★

shirt and breeches.

"Welcome! You made it. Dad will be here in a minute; he's just finishing off a schooling session." The boy's English sounded perfect but he had an unmistakable French accent. Alice wondered if his dad was the resident instructor.

As the boy shook hands with everyone Alice swore that he held on to her hand just a tiny bit longer than the others. He grinned at her – flashing perfect white teeth – and for a moment she found herself unable to speak.

"Alice," the boy repeated softly, as she introduced herself. "*Wonderful* to meet you. I'm Sebastian, or Seb." Then he smiled round at everyone. "Shall I show you the stables?" he said in a charming voice. "Your ponies should be arriving in about half an hour."

"Thank you, Seb." June took charge, organising the group, and everyone trooped behind Seb as he

headed in the direction of the yard. Finn walked next to Alice.

"Finn?" Alice tried to keep her voice low, aware of Holly and Sam right behind them. "Are you OK? You seem a bit … a bit…" She struggled to think of the right word. She didn't want Finn to know she'd overheard his phone conversation the day before.

"A bit what?" Finn snapped. "Yes, Alice, I'm fine."

Alice frowned, but was distracted as they went through the huge ornamental gates leading to the stable yard. They were in an enormous cobbled courtyard with stables down two sides and a huge fountain in the middle. The heady scent of lavender mingled with the hay, and calm horses hung their heads over stable doors.

"How lovely!" June said. "Have you just got the pony club here?"

Seb shook his head. "It's a busy week. We've got fifteen pony clubbers from the UK and we've also got a team from a fashion magazine staying. They're doing a photo shoot with the lavender and they want to include some horses."

"And are all these horses part of the yard?" June asked.

"Not all," Seb replied. "We've actually got other horses staying for the festival. A travelling display team, the Rebel Riders?" He shrugged. "They are a big deal in France."

"Did you say the Rebel Riders?" Finn asked, suddenly sounding very alert.

Seb nodded.

"Oh right," Finn answered. "That *is* cool."

"Who?" Alice whispered as Seb waved to a smartly dressed man who was heading over.

"I'll tell you later," Finn whispered back, but his eyes were sparkling.

The man now shaking June's hand looked like an older version of Seb.

"Hello!" He waved at the group. "I'm Mathis, the resident instructor here. I'm so sorry – I didn't expect you for a few minutes longer. Otherwise I would have been waiting at the gates!"

As he smiled around at the group with an easy charm, Alice instantly felt at ease. It was clear Mathis was a horseman from the way his gorgeous grey horse followed him adoringly back into the stable. According to June, Mathis was one of the best instructors in France.

"So today you'll settle in, and tomorrow the festival begins!" he beamed, and then he looked up as the big silver lorry trundled up the drive. The ponies had arrived!

Alice was soon preoccupied with getting Secret settled. Finn helped the pony club members unload their ponies and stable them in the enormous loose boxes at the end of one of the rows. The stables had windows at both the front and back and despite the heat a breeze fluttered through, keeping the ponies cool. Secret's was the very nearest stable to the yard entrance and Alice hoped she might even be able to see him from her room, like she could at home. It was comforting, having him near. Out of the back window, Alice was gazing at the purple fields again when something caught her eye.

A group of riders were cantering together in the dusty area in front of the lavender rows. All were bareback, some without bridles, on a mixture of horses. As they neared, Alice's eyes were drawn to the woman riding the Arab horse in the lead. She had long dark brown hair flowing behind her, and her posture reminded Alice a little of Sasha.

"Who are they?" She turned round expecting to see Finn, but instead Seb was leaning on her stable door, a dazzling grin on his face. Alice felt a blush

rise up. He was magazine handsome!

"They," Seb replied, "are the Rebel Riders. They're a display team from Spain who travel Europe with their show. They are very good but, between you and me, I like my riding a little more … how do you say … traditional." He gave a lopsided grin. "I prefer to sit on my saddle, not stand!"

Alice couldn't help but smile back. He was gorgeous and his accent was adorable! Then, looking back out of the stable window, she gave a start as she noticed Finn standing between two rows of lavender, hand shielding his eyes from the sun, as he also watched the riders.

★

"So the Rebel Riders are a big deal, right?" Alice sat down next to Finn later in the courtyard. They were having an evening meal after exploring and settling in. Secret was happy in his enormous stable and Alice was planning to ask if she was allowed to ride him once the temperature dropped. She wondered if there was any way Finn could join her, riding one of the yard horses. Perhaps then they could talk while they rode, like they did at home. Something was going on with him, and she knew it was connected to the conversation with his dad that Alice had overheard.

"You can say that again!" Finn replied. "They're amazing. Sasha has all the videos on her laptop, and we always watch them when we're thinking up new routines. They are way above us, though, like leagues above. I've always wanted to see them in action, and now here we are – staying in the same place as them. I can't believe it!"

"That's so cool!" Alice said, thinking about the showjumpers she loved and how amazing it would be to meet them.

Finn nodded. "Isn't it? They've actually asked if I want to go and watch their practice tonight," he

continued. "I told them about the Fillies and they said I can get involved this week when I'm not helping June. I'll do as much as I can with them!"

Alice realised her face must have fallen and she quickly plastered on a smile. *She'd* hoped to spend some special time with Finn during the trip as well. "That's great!" she said in a bright voice. Then she paused. "Are you *sure* you're OK, though, Finn?" Alice asked again.

Finn gave her an exasperated look. "Yes," he said. "I'm sure!" Then his phone beeped, and, pulling it out, his face darkened.

"Who's that?" Alice asked, and Finn shot her an annoyed look.

"No one."

Just then a new group of people arrived and sat at the tables next to them. Alice couldn't help but stare. They *really* didn't look like horsey people! Despite the heat, they were mostly wearing black and everyone was wearing huge sunglasses. They had to be the fashion magazine team. Noticing Alice looking at them, the lady nearest to her pushed her sunglasses up and glared at her with very green eyes. She was quite young, perhaps in her mid-twenties.

"Yes?" she snapped. "Can I help?"

Finn raised his eyebrows.

The lady next to her frowned. "Maria, be nice. They're just pony club kids." Then, leaning forward, she gave a little wave. Alice smiled shyly. She recognised her; she was sure of it. Her pale hair was pulled back into a neat chignon and she had an heart-shaped face. Diamond bracelets round her slim wrists sparkled as she moved her hands.

"I was in a pony club when I was your age," she smiled. "You'll have to introduce me to your ponies! I'm Gabby, by the way. This is Maria."

Alice was sure she hadn't met Gabby before but

she seemed so familiar, perhaps she just reminded her of someone else?

The rude lady, Maria, gave a snort and grimaced. "Rather you than me," she said. "Quite frankly, the further we stay from those horrid creatures, the better. It's bad enough having to get up close and personal to them in the shoots."

Gabby grinned and rolled her eyes behind Maria's back, making Alice laugh. She promised Gabby she would introduce her to Secret. But turning back to chat to Finn, Alice gave a start. He'd gone.

Chapter 4

A few minutes after Finn's sudden departure, Holly joined Alice at the table. The super-friendly girl had already got to know all of the girls from the other pony club branches who'd arrived during the day, and waved for them to come over.

"Alice!" she squealed. "This is Lizzie, Beth, Jenny and Ellen! Isn't this so exciting?"

And, despite wondering why Finn had

disappeared so suddenly, Alice felt content. It was really nice to meet the other girls and chat about the festival and their ponies. It turned out Beth's pony Buzz was stabled next to Secret.

"I met Secret just now," Beth said in a soft Welsh accent. "He's gorgeous!" Alice swelled with pride. "Just watch Buzz," Beth continued. "She can nip, but she's all talk mostly!"

"Sounds like Minstrel! Small pony syndrome!" Holly laughed. Her Shetland cross Welsh pony was on the other side of Buzz. The rest of the meal was full of laughter and pony chat and Alice loved every second.

She went to see Secret once they'd finished dinner. Mathis had promised the pony clubbers they could turn their ponies out in the shaded paddocks surrounding the yard, but Secret seemed happy in his huge space and Alice was pleased that she'd remembered to pack his special door clip.

She'd never live it down if he escaped! Crossing the yard towards the tack room, she jumped as she almost walked straight into Seb, who was carrying a bridle over his arm.

"Hey, Alice!" Seb grinned at her. He looked super handsome in his riding kit.

She gave a little awkward wave in response. "Hey!"

"Where's your friend Finn?" Seb continued, leaning against the whitewashed wall.

"Oh." Alice hesitated. "I think he's hanging out with the Rebel Riders."

Seb raised an eyebrow. "Interesting," he said. "They usually keep themselves to themselves."

"Finn rides in a display team at home, with his sister," Alice explained. "He's good. Really good," she added.

"Hmmm," Seb said dismissively, then grinned his heart-stoppingly gorgeous grin. "It's a beautiful

evening," he said, gesturing at the sky that was a hazy mixture of turquoise and pink. The heat had gone out of the day, and it was balmy and peaceful. "Would you like to come for a ride with me, and I'll show you around?"

Alice smiled. She'd been longing to ride around the estate ever since they'd arrived. "That would be lovely," she replied.

"Meet me out here in ten minutes." Seb grinned at her again, and then he was gone.

★

Alice had expected Seb to be riding a pony, but he led out a beautiful dark brown warmblood mare, who was well over sixteen hands. She was so tall that Alice had to look up at Seb as they rode side by side, turning up the dusty track that wound its way through the lavender.

Seb's mare wore a lot of tack. There was a complicated bridle with a grackle noseband

and martingale and boots on all four legs. Seb had on expensive-looking long shiny boots and spurs, the type Alice saw on the showjumpers at Hickstead. Alice looked down at Secret's bridle. He had a simple snaffle with plaited reins, and the oiled leather felt cool and familiar in her hands. Josephine was a firm believer in as little tack as possible and, with Finn and Alice, had overhauled the tack room one quiet day, getting rid of any unnecessary gadgets. It had made Alice so happy to see her mum and Finn really working together.

"Your horse is lovely," Alice said, unable to think of anything else to say. "And quite big."

"Yes, I've never really bothered with ponies." Seb smiled down at her. "If you want to compete with the other riders, a good horse is the way forward! I'll leave the ponies to the amateurs."

Alice raised an eyebrow. "Ponies have just as much going for them," she said loyally. "And

believe me," she added, thinking of her past struggles, "just because they're smaller doesn't make them easier!"

Secret was feeling a little fresh, and skipped along beside Seb's mare as if proving Alice's point.

"What's her name?" Alice felt slightly breathless, trying to stop Secret from cantering off. He was having to jog to keep up with the warmblood's long strides.

"Clea," Seb replied.

"Pretty name," Alice said. "It suits her."

"I guess." Seb shrugged. "I didn't name her. I'm more interested in what she can do."

"Oh." Alice felt taken aback.

"She's got this season to prove herself, and if not, she'll be sold on," Seb continued. "I want to make it as a professional, get sponsorship. So, I need the right machine."

"Er, right." Alice had never heard a horse referred

to as a machine before.

Seeing her expression, Seb chuckled. "Alice, it's a business," he said, and she frowned. Seb was more or less the same age as her, and yet he was speaking to her as if he was a grown-up and she was a child! "I can't afford to ride horses who aren't producing results."

Alice nodded, although she couldn't imagine selling Secret just because he wasn't capable of doing exactly what she wanted.

"Dad doesn't think like me," Seb said. "He'd keep every horse if he could. But I want to make a name for myself. The festival is a good opportunity to prove myself and the prize money is excellent, so if I win a few classes I can put it towards another horse or two."

Alice thought about the money she'd won in the past. The average was about twenty pounds, enough for a few treats for herself and Secret.

Seb must be talking *big* prize money.

"Oh," she said. "Sounds like a lot?"

"The winner of my big class gets ten thousand euros," Seb continued airily. "You pony clubbers—" there was something about the way he said this that made Alice frown again— "your class is pretty good as well. About eleven hundred euros. That's, what, about one thousand pounds?"

A thousand pounds! *That's a fortune*, Alice thought, her imagination starting to run away with her. She had her eye on some amazing blue stirrups her mum flatly refused to buy, and a new riding hat with tiny diamantes on the peak, just like she'd seen at Hickstead. She imagined herself going on a wild shopping spree at the local saddlery.

They'd reached the top of the lavender rows now and beyond them the land stretched out, yellow and dusty. Alice looked back at the stable courtyard shining white among the purple. It was beautiful, and she told Seb so.

"Isn't it?" Seb looked down at her and smiled. "Even better when I have beautiful company to enjoy it with."

Alice felt herself blush right up to the roots of her hair, and Seb chuckled. "Come on," he said. "Race you along the ridge!"

Alice let Secret have his head. As they cantered along, hooves sending up clouds of soft, sandy dust, Alice laughed out loud. She still had to pinch herself that she was actually here!

Alice woke up early the next morning. She and Holly were sharing a room in the chateau. The house was like a maze, and they had already got lost so many times, giggling as they kept turning down the wrong corridor, apologising to the fashion team as they accidentally found themselves in the smartest wing where they were staying.

Pulling on a pair of shorts and a vest top, Alice wandered down to the stables, ready to muck out. Their first lesson was after breakfast, and she couldn't wait to get stuck in.

"Hey again, Alice!" Beth, the Welsh girl she'd met the day before waved cheerfully. Buzz was tied up and making all sorts of funny faces. "Ah, now," Beth said, chiding her pony gently. "Be nice!"

Alice chuckled and set to work on her own stable, chatting to Beth and Holly who'd just appeared.

"Psssst, Alice!" Holly grinned, peering round the stable door. Alice was just sweeping up the last of the shavings as Secret finished his breakfast. "Did you go riding with Seb last night?"

"Seb?" Beth had now joined Holly. "Ooh! Lucky you!"

Alice blushed. "Well, yeah. I mean, Secret needed a leg stretch. And Seb offered, and he knows his way around…" Her voice trailed off.

"A leg stretch?!" Beth giggled. "Nice work, Alice! He's gorgeous!"

"No … I mean, yes he is … is he?" Alice felt tongue-tied but Holly smiled kindly.

"Hey, we're only teasing!" she grinned. "But I could tell he liked you straight away!"

To Alice's relief, Secret bustled forward to say hello to someone walking past. It was Gabby, the lady from the magazine, clutching a cup of coffee, which Secret almost spilled as he gave her shoulder a nudge. Gabby laughed, setting her coffee down so she could say hello to him properly.

"Sorry," Alice apologised. "He's a bit over-friendly at times."

Gabby smiled, still stroking Secret. "It's made my morning!" she said brightly, and Alice smiled back.

"We're just about to do one of our shoots," Gabby continued. She didn't seem to mind one bit

that Secret was leaving red hairs all over her crisp white shirt. "And I'd forgotten just how nice it is to hang out at some stables!"

Alice watched in interest as a beautiful girl strolled into the yard surrounded by assistants. She had smooth caramel skin and her dark hair was in a long plait, and she was wearing the most incredible white gown.

"Is that a *wedding* dress?" Alice blurted out.

Gabby smiled. "It is! We're doing a whole feature on them," she said. "And here's our lovely horse."

One of the grooms was tying up a beautiful grey outside a stable. The horse was wearing an ornate bridle decorated with little silver bells.

Maria, appearing next to them, tossed back her dark hair and scowled. "A bit OTT? I still think this shoot would work perfectly well without that creature."

"As I said *before*, it will be amazing," Gabby

replied, sounding irritated.

Maria rolled her eyes and stalked off, and Gabby frowned, her lips pursed.

Alice mentally crossed her fingers that Gabby would get the photos she wanted with the beautiful grey. Anything to get one over on pony-hating Maria!

"There you are," the groom said in broken English. "He's all yours. He's a good boy, one of the quiet ones. You said you had some horse experience? Are you happy to take over from here?"

"Thank you – yes, that's fine." Gabby smiled at the groom who went on with his yard work as the horse rested a leg and looked around him calmly.

Suddenly more people appeared: a photographer, a couple of assistants, and someone carrying some heavy-looking equipment. Gabby was consulting her notebook, while the crew was heaving boxes

of props around and the model was checking her phone in a shady corner.

Alice turned back to Secret as the fashion team bustled around. Then suddenly there was a shriek and a clatter of hooves and everyone jumped as the grey horse, now loose, careered over the cobbles past Maria, who cowered behind a big suitcase.

"Help!" she cried dramatically. "That thing almost killed me!"

With no one else moving Alice started to come out of Secret's stable, knowing someone needed to try to catch the loose horse. His reins were broken, dangling down to his legs, and this seemed to panic him, causing him to career into a large box of equipment, knocking it to the ground with a crash and spilling props all over the yard. This in turn spooked the horse even more as he kicked out at a light reflector. He was in a complete frenzy.

Just then Finn appeared from the other side of

the yard, close to the big grey. Using the same body language he'd used when Secret had been loose at the country fair all those months ago, he approached the horse calmly and had hold of his bridle in no time, patting him and reassuring him as he led him back past the equipment.

"He seems a bit spooked by all this stuff," Finn explained, looking at all the gear in the yard. "Poor boy."

"See!" Maria hissed at Gabby who was looking all around at the fallen equipment. "I told you it wouldn't work! They do say never work with children *or* animals!"

Alice frowned. Closing the stable door behind her and moving closer to the now calm horse she saw that the break in his reins was neat, as if it had been cut.

"Look at this," she said. "It looks like someone cut the reins!"

Maria glared at her. "Don't be ridiculous! The creature broke free! He's clearly wild. I don't think we can use him; it's not safe."

Finn looked at Maria as if she were crazy and shook his head. "He's not wild! He just had a fright and needs to adjust to the equipment. What about if I gave you a hand on the shoot? It might take longer than you had planned, though."

"That would be amazing," Gabby said gratefully.

But Maria just looked furious. "Time is money, Gabby – you know that!" she hissed. "As art director, if we don't get the shots in time, this all falls on me!"

"It'll be fine. I'll take responsibility as *editor* of the magazine," Gabby said calmly, before turning to Finn. "Thank you. Finn, isn't it?"

"That's right." Finn stroked the grey on his neck and started to lead him out of the yard. Glancing at Maria, Alice felt a shiver run down her spine.

Maria wore a look of pure hatred as she followed Finn and Gabby, who were now chatting away as they headed out towards the lavender.

Chapter 5

Alice soon had other things on her mind. It turned out that Secret had made himself busy during the night. Each stable had its own beautifully hand-painted number on a slightly raised box sign. Alice realised Secret had chewed and peeled the sign's woodwork so much that she could almost slide one finger behind it!

"Secret!" she scolded him, and he blinked

innocently at her. Alice went to find Mathis to tell him what Secret had been up to.

"Well now," Mathis said in an amused tone as he inspected the damage, "we've never had a pony do that."

"Sorry," Alice mumbled. "You've probably not had a pony like Secret before."

Mathis laughed. "He's certainly got a glint in his eye! There's not much point moving him; all the stables have the same sign." He looked thoughtful. "We have a product that will help – it tastes horrid and should stop him chewing. I'll put some on the sign."

"Sorry again," Alice called as Mathis went off to find some. "And as for you—" she turned to her Welsh pony affectionately— "can you just *try* to stay out of trouble?"

★

After breakfast with the rest of the pony club

members, minus Finn, Alice was back out at the stables tacking up Secret. The little pony looked most put out that foul-smelling brown liquid had been smeared on the sign and spoilt his fun!

The fifteen pony clubbers were divided into three groups, and Alice was in Mathis's group to start. Holly, Beth and Lizzie were also in her group. As they circled the arena Alice could see the yellow and white circus tents in the distance. She couldn't wait to explore later!

Secret snorted a little, eyeing up the brightly painted showjumps. Soon the group were trotting and cantering on both reins, before jumping over the grid exercise Mathis had set up. Secret bounded around with glee, launching himself over the jumps as though he was rocket-propelled. She noticed that a couple of pony club members from other branches were also struggling to control fresh ponies.

Mathis soon had the riders going back to basics, as Angus did at the pony club, and as they cantered over poles on the ground she relaxed as Secret started to calm down.

"OK!" Mathis gathered them into the centre of the arena. He seemed sharper today, more business-like, as he clapped his hands. "We have lots to work on. The competition at the end of the week will be fierce, and I want you all to be riding at your best. Although it is a pony club class, the standards are high, and so are the jumps! Now, do you all know what a top score class is?"

Alice nodded, feeling her tummy lurch. A top score class was where each jump was awarded points based on how difficult it was, and the competitors could choose their own route around the course. The most difficult fence in the course with the most points was known as the joker, and the competitors had to decide whether or not to

risk jumping it. Alice had watched similar classes at county shows over the years and knew it was fast and furious … and totally up Secret's street!

The rest of the lesson went well and Alice was cooling Secret down when she saw Mathis wave to someone just outside the arena. Following his gaze, Alice gave a start as she noticed Seb leaning against the arena fence. She hadn't seen him watching the lesson.

"Your pony looks a handful," Seb commented as Alice rode back out. "Well ridden."

Alice immediately felt defensive. She hated other people pointing out Secret's quirks, even Finn and Angus. But Seb had also complimented her, and his smile was so dazzling that Alice couldn't help but smile back. "He can be tricky," she admitted. "But I know him well."

Seb fell into step with her as she walked Secret back up to the yard. It was growing hot, and Alice hoped she'd be able to take a dip in the swimming pool soon.

"What about a ride this evening?" Seb continued. "When the schools are free?"

"OK!" Alice couldn't help feeling excited at the thought of spending time with Seb. And, knowing now what the final competition was comprised of, she and Secret could do with as much practice as possible. Alice really wanted to do well, to represent her branch *and* justify her place on the trip.

"Looking forward to it," Seb replied, but as Alice dismounted Secret she caught the back of her heel on a cobble and stumbled, falling straight into Seb's arms, who stopped her from falling flat on the floor. "Whoa!" he laughed. "Good thing I was here to save your life!"

"My hero!" Alice replied back with a smile, mentally high-fiving herself for such a quick retort.

A PONY called SECRET

And that's when Finn strode back into the yard, leading the big grey from the photo shoot. Alice immediately jumped apart from Seb, who grinned.

"Finn!" Alice said a little too quickly. "How did it go with the photos?"

"Fine."

There was an awkward silence before Gabby came in behind them, trailed by several assistants holding bags, a relieved smile on her face.

"Finn was brilliant!" she exclaimed. "He's a natural! With his help I think we got the shots. It took a little longer than we thought, but I'm sure the photos will be amazing."

"Well, we'll see, won't we?" Maria muttered as she strutted past, carrying a box between her hands like it was the Crown Jewels. "Quite why we had to have horses in the photos, Gabby, is beyond me."

"Because it's a core part of the artistic direction

for the feature, Maria. That's the whole point of us being here," Gabby replied firmly. "Trust me, they'll be special."

Although Gabby was the boss, Maria didn't seem to have any respect for her, Alice thought. It was weird!

As Maria passed Secret, she arched her body away from him as if he was a snake. When his soft muzzle nudged the box she was holding Maria shrieked, flapping a hand at him. Secret put his ears back, a wounded look on his handsome face.

"Stay away!" Maria hissed. "There's a very valuable necklace in this box. Worth a hundred of you, horrid pony!"

"He's *not* horrid!" Alice responded crossly, gently pulling Secret's reins back. Alice decided she *really* didn't like Maria. As far as she was concerned, Secret was priceless, far more valuable than any piece of jewellery!

Chapter 6

A little later, Alice and Finn walked back up to the yard together after turning Secret out. "Sounds like you did a great job on the shoot," Alice said to Finn.

He shrugged. "It wasn't hard."

"So what were the Rebel Riders like yesterday?" Alice asked, and Finn's face lit up.

"So cool," he enthused. "Like, how they think

up their routines, and the training they give their horses. If I could just take back a little bit of what I learn, it would make the Fillies even better... That's if..."

It looked like he was going to say something else and then he stopped, his voice trailing off.

"What about the Fillies?"

Finn opened his mouth to reply but then Seb appeared, carrying a glass of iced water for Alice.

"I thought you might like a cool drink," he said in a charming voice. "Looking forward to seeing you later!"

"Er, thanks." Alice took the water, as Seb strolled off.

Finn looked at her. "He seems friendly," he said, and Alice couldn't work out his tone.

She frowned. "Well, yeah. Everyone is so nice. Well, apart from Maria! Anyway, *what* were you going to say about the Fillies?"

Finn gave her the same exasperated look he'd used the previous day. "Oh, it's nothing," he mumbled, a note of annoyance creeping into his voice.

"Money stuff?" Alice pressed, remembering what she'd overheard.

"Stuff that's between *me* and *Sash* and *Dad!*" Finn sounded really cross now, and Alice frowned at him.

"Look," Finn said more softly, "we'll catch up later, OK? I'm going to go and chill out in my room. The Rebel Riders have asked me to join them later, when it's a bit cooler, so I'm off to look at some of their old routines online."

As Finn strode off, Alice sighed. They'd only been at the centre for a day, and it felt like they were having completely different experiences...

★

A few hours later, after enjoying a swim with

Holly in the pool and lounging in the sun, Alice went to bring Secret back in from his paddock. The day was still warm, but the ferociousness of the midday heat had dispersed, and Secret ambled over, having enjoyed his doze underneath the trees.

As she took Secret to his stable, Alice noticed that the magazine team were setting up a new shoot in the yard opposite. Another of the centre's horses was being used, this time a beautiful palomino mare, who reminded Alice of Secret's dam, the gorgeous Lily. The horse stood quietly as the model posed next to her, one arm draped over her creamy mane.

Holly joined Alice and together they watched the pictures being taken.

"Perfect!" Gabby called, and then, seeing the girls watching, gave them a wave. They waved shyly back, watching as the next photo was set up.

Maria, who was rifling through racks of expensive-looking clothes, glared in their direction, and Alice frowned. They weren't doing anything wrong by just standing there! They were close enough to hear what was being said as Maria stood up, hands on hips.

"Gabby?" she said in a loaded voice. "That dress we need to shoot. It's not here."

Gabby turned round with a frown. "What do you mean?" she said. "I organised the clothes myself."

"I mean exactly what I said," Maria huffed. "It's not here. Perhaps it's been lost. Or *stolen*. There are kids all over the place." She gave Alice and Holly an accusing look. "So what do we do now? It's a one-off piece! You know we *have* to include it."

"It won't have been stolen, Maria." Gabby sounded cross. "It'll be here somewhere."

Feeling a bit awkward, Alice and Holly started to creep away, but paused as Sam went hurrying over to Maria and Gabby, clutching something in his hand. Alice moved closer to him, trying to work out what he was holding.

"Um," he said hesitantly. "Is this yours?"

Maria snatched the item from his hand, holding it out so that everyone could see a shimmering pink dress, crumpled and covered in straw and shavings.

"Where did you find this?" Maria said in an accusing voice, and Sam shrugged. "It was where all the mucking-out tools are kept," he said. "I don't know how it got there."

Gabby took the dress. "Thanks for returning it," she said kindly. "That's a bit of a mystery…" For a minute she looked worried, as if trying to decide what to do. "*How* can we shoot this now?" she added almost to herself. "We *have* to feature this dress in next month's issue…"

Suddenly Alice had an idea. She didn't read

glossy magazines very often but when she flicked through them it always made her smile to see photos of models in extraordinary clothes apparently doing normal, everyday things, like walking dogs or gardening. Maybe something similar would work here? She liked Gabby and decided if she could help her, she should.

"Um, just a thought…" she blurted out before she had second thoughts, "but what about if the model is supposed to be *helping* with the horses? Then there'd be a few shavings and a bit of dirt on the dress and all around her? It could be made part of the whole thing? Maybe?"

Gabby paused for a moment and then turned to Alice, eyes sparkling.

"That's it!" she cried. "The shoot will be all about a day at the stables – with everything that entails! We'll use the dress; even if it is a bit crumpled it's still stunning." She laughed, clearly relieved.

"Remind me of the jobs you do in a yard; it's been so long since I cared for a pony!"

"Um…" Alice thought. "Mucking out? Grooming? Filling water buckets? Cleaning tack?"

Gabby clapped. "Perfect! Anna," she called to the model, "are you up for a bit of horse-care?"

The dark-haired girl nodded. "Sure!"

And that was that. Gabby started to direct the crew – setting up shots that involved the model supposedly mucking out the palomino, grooming and cleaning tack, wearing a selection of designer dresses and sparkling jewels.

Gabby grinned. "I think these shots are going to be sensational!"

Holly, who was still watching with Sam, nudged Alice, chuckling. "Well done, Al! They should give you a job!"

"Er, no." Alice grinned back. "I'll stick to my ponies, thanks!"

And with the shoot in full swing Alice, Sam and Holly turned to leave, but not before Alice saw Maria throw a look of pure hatred at Gabby. It was so venomous that a shiver went down Alice's spine. What *was* her problem?

★

Leaving the stables, Alice climbed up through the lavender until she reached the meadow. It was nice to be in the peace and quiet after the craziness of the fashion team and their shoot. What a strange world! Sitting down in the shade of a tree, she watched as the Rebel Riders and Finn laughed and joked as they warmed up. Finn was riding a beautiful black pony in his usual relaxed style. Once again, Alice's eyes were drawn to the leader of the group. Alice thought she must be in her early twenties. She was as striking as the model from the shoot earlier but in a wilder way, her long dark hair flowing behind her as she cantered bareback.

The group gathered together and moments later Finn set off at a gallop and threw himself off the side of the saddle, stretching back and down towards the ground as his head almost brushed the dusty earth. It was one of the tricks he performed with the Flying Fillies. The Rebel Riders looked impressed.

"Great!" The leader of the group gave a clap. Her voice was clear and strong. "I can see there's not much we need to teach you."

Finn smiled such a rare, genuine smile that Alice felt her stomach flip. She thought about Seb and his perfect white grin. Somehow it just didn't seem as sincere.

Alice gave a start as she realised the woman was trotting towards her on her horse, a gorgeous steel-grey gelding with a mane rippling down to his powerful shoulders. The woman was dressed simply in a linen shirt dress, and her skin was

smooth and brown.

"Hello, I'm Celia." In one smooth movement she had hopped down from the back of the horse, and then, to Alice's fascination, the woman gestured towards the ground and the big horse lay down next to her. "And this is Domino," she added with a grin. "You must be Alice?"

"Yes, that's me." Alice was suddenly aware her voice sounded a bit squeaky. Celia was so cool that it was slightly terrifying!

"Finn was telling me who he came here with," Celia continued. "Is your pony that cute little roan?" Alice nodded. "He's got some spark in him; I like him."

"Thank you!" Alice couldn't stop the grin spreading over her face.

"I'd better get back to it – I just wanted to come and say hi!" Celia mounted the horse while he was still lying down and clicked her tongue. The horse stretched and then rose to his feet, Celia perfectly balanced on his back.

For the next hour Alice sat in the dappled sunlight and watched the Rebel Riders. They had a wild energy about them, the horses and riders all equally as striking. Some wore tack, jewelled bridles and intricately embroidered side-saddles, and others, like Celia's horse, just a simple rope round their shiny necks.

As the riders performed trick after trick, each one more daring than the last, jumping lavender rows while standing on the horses' backs, vaulting on at full gallop, Alice thought about the showjumping world, all plaited manes and flashy jackets and sparkling stock pins. This was the polar opposite. It was Finn's world, and he'd never looked so alive.

Chapter 7

Once all the display horses were warmed down, Finn rode over to Alice. He looked totally relaxed.

"That was brilliant!" she said, and Finn smiled.

"Thanks," he said, shaking back his dark hair, which was damp with sweat.

"Sasha will be so jealous!" Alice continued, trying not to think about how gorgeous Finn looked, and he gave her a half-smile. "You'll have to show her what you learn here, and put it all in the Flying Fillies routines!" Alice chattered on, then stopped as a dark look flashed across Finn's face. "What? What is it, Finn?"

Finn looked away. "Nothing."

Alice frowned. Every time she mentioned the Flying Fillies, Finn clammed up. It was so annoying.

"What IS up?" she tried again. "Is the yard in trouble?"

Finn gave her another exasperated look. "The yard's always in trouble!" he said. "It's nothing new! We need money and we need it fast."

Alice thought quickly, wanting to help her friend. "Well, you've got all that space... What about livery? Or training other people's horses?"

Finn shook his head. "It wouldn't work," he said in an irritated voice. "Can you imagine anyone wanting to let their precious horses live in our

tumbledown old yard?"

"I think it's beautiful," Alice said loyally. Rookham Manor still took her breath away, from the honey-coloured stone to the meadows full of wildflowers. She knew the fencing was rotten and the walls were crumbling, but to her it was the most romantic place ever.

"Yes, but beautiful doesn't pay the bills," Finn said darkly. "And anyway, we don't have time to think of anything. When I say fast, I mean we need the money *now*."

Alice thought about the phone conversation that she'd overheard … and then an idea popped into her head. Finn had said that he desperately needed £1,000 to help save the yard. What if Alice won the showjumping competition? She could give the prize money to Finn! She opened her mouth to blurt this out and then closed it again, needing more time to think through her plan.

As they headed back down to the yard the silence between them was soon interrupted by a cheerful shout.

"Alice!"

It was Seb, sauntering over and looking dashing in stone-coloured breeches and a dark navy polo shirt. "I've been looking all over for you. Ready to ride?"

"Oh! Yes, of course." Alice had forgotten about her schooling session with Seb. "I'll just go and get changed and get Secret ready."

"Can't wait." Seb winked at her, and Alice blushed.

"See you later, Finn?" She glanced up at him, but his face was blank.

"OK," he said. Then, as Seb strolled off towards Clea, Finn frowned. "I saw him ride yesterday. You know, he approaches things very differently to Dad." He spoke in a low voice. "I mean, I know

he does well in the competitions, but is his style really for you? It's very ... cold."

"He's only watching me school," Alice retorted, feeling irritated. "What's wrong with that?" She wanted the extra practice, especially now the plan to win the prize money for Finn was buzzing around in her head.

But Finn just looked at her. "Nothing, I guess." But his tone suggested otherwise.

★

"So, are you and Finn good friends at home?" Seb asked casually as they walked side by side to the arena, Alice leading Secret.

"Well, yes. I guess. I mean, yeah, we are." Alice felt a little flustered. It was always hard to explain her relationship with Finn. They had a connection, something special. But when Finn put his defences up, as he was doing at the moment, it was almost impossible to get through to him.

"He seems ... reserved," Seb said. "Quite moody, no?"

"Oh, no, not really." Alice tried to stick up for him. "I suppose a bit, but only if you don't know him that well."

"He's not full of sunshine, like you." Seb looked straight at her and once again Alice felt the dreaded blush rise up.

"He's fine," she said quickly. "He just has some things going on at home."

"What sort of things?" Seb seemed genuinely interested.

"Oh," Alice replied vaguely, thinking about Rookham Manor, "just some financial troubles with his yard. Bills and things."

"Horses are expensive," Seb said after a pause, and Alice nodded. She was sure Seb understood Finn's money troubles. After all, Seb had to find sponsorship to become a professional rider.

"Right then." Seb stood back as Alice swung lightly into Secret's saddle. "Let's see you ride!"

Alice had changed into one of her new sleeveless shirts, and with her long ponytail swinging behind her in rhythm with Secret's strides, she hoped Seb was impressed with how she and Secret looked together. Alice hoped Seb was impressed with how *she* looked too. There was something about the way he held her gaze for just longer than was normal that sent shivers down her spine.

Seb set up a few jumps, and Alice and Secret flew over them. Unlike other ponies who tired after jumping, the more Secret jumped the more alive he became and Alice was soon having to cling on tight.

"You need more," Seb said, raising the jumps a few holes. "Give him something to think about."

Alice swallowed hard, but nudged Secret on. The height was taller than she was used to, but

Secret was more than capable, and she wanted to impress Seb. Sensing her change of mood, Secret started cantering sideways, pulling Alice into the jump. He leapt over it and pulled her on to the next fence.

Alice felt the familiar sense of losing control, but she remembered Angus's words about sitting up, not interfering with Secret's mouth and trusting him. And so she went with him and he settled, leaping each jump with effortless grace. Finally, after several laps of the enormous arena, Secret slowed, and Alice gave him a delighted pat.

Seb had a quizzical look on his face. "Well," he said, "he can jump. But why do you let him get away with that? He is in charge and you are just a passenger. He's rude."

Alice frowned. She thought they'd done brilliantly.

"I don't let him get away with it! He loves

jumping and gets excited. He always has, and he probably always will," she said crossly. "Things have improved a *lot* actually."

Seb frowned. "You need to do more. Why are you riding him in such a soft bit? He's taking advantage of you."

Alice looked down. Secret was gazing away into the distance. His snaffle bit shone in the evening sun.

"It's what I've always ridden him in," she replied. "We've been working on my riding and our relationship rather than changing my tack."

Seb chuckled and shook his head. "Listen, your pony is talented. I like him. He could be jumping the biggest tracks, if you could just control him a little better."

Alice thought about this. Her ambitions hadn't really stretched beyond the pony club team just yet, but she knew Secret was capable of more.

"I guess, but he's young, and he's got years to improve," she said.

"What about the competition?" Seb asked. "You surely want to do well, don't you? Who knows where it could lead you..."

Alice nodded. "I actually really want to win," she blurted out before she could stop herself.

"Ambition, I like that!" Seb said. "So, listen, I know how this competition will go. I watch it every year. Let's go for it! We'll have a few more sessions together. I'll help you!"

Alice nodded, feeling pleased to have Seb on her side.

★

Holly, Sam and a few other pony clubbers were hanging out in the courtyard later on as Alice finished untacking Secret.

Sam waved her over and she joined the group.

"We're all going to head down to the festival

and see what's going on," he explained. "Want to come?"

Alice nodded eagerly. She loved being part of this gang. She'd always been on the edge of groups at school.

"Sure!" she grinned. "Give me five minutes. I'll invite Finn as well."

"Of course! The more the merrier," Sam said, nodding. "We'll wait here for you."

Alice sprinted back to the stables to where Finn was reading a book in the shade.

"Hey," she said a little breathlessly. "We're heading down to the festival. Want to come with us?"

Finn turned down the corner of the page he was reading and shielded the sun from his eyes as he looked up. "No, not really."

"Why not?" Alice said in surprise. "It'll be fun."

Finn shrugged. "Just don't fancy it." He picked

up his book again and deliberately held it up in front of his face to carry on reading. "Have fun."

"Suit yourself," Alice snapped before sprinting back to the others. Honestly – Finn was infuriating!

The festival, just a five-minute walk from the centre, was teeming with activity. The trade stands were busy, and delicious smells wafted over from the food tents. A Shetland Grand National heat was going on in the main ring to the delight of the cheering crowd. Alice was having so much fun with the others, she'd almost forgotten about Finn. That is, until she and Beth sat down to watch a jousting competition, and her mind wandered back to him as the horses thundered up and down the turf.

Finn would really enjoy this, she thought, frowning. She decided she would go and find him in a bit. But a few minutes later, watching the first of the showjumping classes, Alice was completely

transfixed, and Finn slipped from her mind once more. *This* was the world she wanted to be part of. It was an adult class and the competition was fast and furious, each rider taking more risks than the last, turning hairpin corners, jumping huge oxers from just one stride out to the delight of the cheering crowd. The sun had dropped and the Ferris wheel was illuminated against a pink evening sky as the winner of the class, a young woman on a gorgeous big bay, cantered around. Clapping until her hands hurt, Alice didn't think she'd felt as happy in a long time.

★

The next morning, Alice bumped into Finn on her way to muck out and told him all about the festival. The pony clubbers were about to go off on a hack together, but they had some free time later on and she hoped she could spend it with Finn.

"You should come down to the festival today,"

she said hopefully. "The medieval jousting yesterday was amazing. And I think they have the Prince Philip Cup games today. You could headhunt the next Flying Fillies member!"

She meant it as a joke, but noticed Finn's eyes darkened when she mentioned the Fillies.

"Or we could just hang out," she said, her voice quieter.

But Finn shrugged. "We'll see. Depends." And he headed off without any further conversation.

Alice stared at his departing back with a growing sense of irritation. Surely he could at least try to get involved, *try* to have fun? There was no point asking if he wanted to come along on the hack; he'd only say no.

Her thoughts were interrupted by Gabby coming into the yard, greeting each pony in turn. She seemed to know all their names already.

"Hello, Secret!" She gave the little roan a pat.

"Hello, Alice. I have to say the pictures from yesterday were *brilliant*! Thank you so much! Now, have you seen Finn?"

"He's gone off somewhere," Alice said, slightly surprised. "Why?"

"We've got a couple of shoots we want to do today with the horse, out in the fields," Gabby explained. "He was so helpful last time! If you see him, perhaps you could ask him to come and find me?"

"OK," Alice agreed. "You must do lots of exciting things in your job," she said after a pause, watching Gabby pat Secret.

"Yes, I'm very lucky," Gabby smiled. "This week is a particularly big week for me. I've only just become editor of the magazine, and the photos we're taking this week will star in a big 'summer weddings' feature. It's important that they are perfect, and so far it's looking good, with your and

Finn's help!"

"No problem," Alice said. "I hope the rest go well!"

"Fingers crossed!" Gabby said, and then her smile faded as Maria strode up, sunglasses on, dressed in her regular uniform of black. She wrinkled her nose as she approached the stables, and Alice frowned. The smell of hay and horses was heaven to her!

"Gabby," she said shortly, completely ignoring Alice. "Dan has been emailing me. He wants to see some more stills, and you haven't got back to him. I had to tell him I'd come and find you *again*."

Her tone was icy, and Gabby frowned. "He only emailed half an hour ago," she said.

Maria rolled her eyes. "Quite honestly, I'll be glad to get out of here. I'm fed up with horses and kids everywhere and *you* getting distracted by the wretched creatures all the time." And with that

Maria spun on her high heels and was gone.

Alice coughed a little awkwardly.

"Sorry about that," Gabby said, and her voice lowered. "She's a little … intense." She sighed. "Stick to horses, Alice! Far less complicated than people."

"Oh, I will."

Alice meant it, and Secret nudged her, as if in agreement.

Chapter 8

The morning hack was brilliant, the perfect chance to really get to know the other pony clubbers as they wound their way up into the forest. Talk had mostly been about the upcoming competition, and there was already a buzz in the air. And as bad as she felt for thinking it, Alice was almost glad Finn wasn't there as she laughed and joked with her new friends. Secret was happy and relaxed as Alice

turned him out into the paddock on her return and she watched for a moment as he rolled.

Then she spotted something at the same time as Secret, and her heart sank. The gate on the other side of the paddock was open, and Secret was trotting purposely across to investigate. He could sense immediately if there were any escape routes nearby.

"No, no, no!" Alice muttered under her breath as she jogged across the paddock. She didn't want to start chasing him, as he would turn it into a game, but she *had* to reach the gate before him.

"Come on, Secret!" she pleaded. "You've stayed out of trouble for three days…"

Too late. With a joyful kick of his heels Secret was through the gate and cantering up through the rows of lavender that lay beyond the paddock. Alice broke into a run. Ahead was a whole crew of people, a model in a particularly elaborate layered wedding dress, and the entire magazine team along with high-tech camera equipment and lighting. And Secret was trotting straight through the middle of it.

Had Alice not been panicking, she might have appreciated that Secret was looking his best – the characteristic Welsh trot more exaggerated than ever, his red mane and tail fanned behind him, and his strong neck arched. As he reached the team they scattered, and Alice heard Maria screech. Secret had poked his nose straight through the big reflector, tearing the material with an audible rip until he'd pushed his whole head through.

Giving a comedy spook, he backed up, shaking the reflector free and sending a tripod flying, before heading over to a table set up with make-up and accessories, shoving his muzzle into the pots and blowing gold dust everywhere as he snorted, his whiskers coated in fine glitter. To Alice's horror

she felt a giggle rise up and tried to supress it. This was so terrible she felt a little hysterical.

"Secret, stop!" She made another desperate attempt to catch him as Secret picked up a piece of silver material in his teeth and swung it around.

Alice realised the material was another expensive-looking dress, no doubt now adorned with a mix of red hairs, green pony slobber and gold dust.

"Secret, put that down! Come HERE!" Alice shouted. Surely it couldn't get any worse ... but then to her horror Maria ran over, flapping her hands and waving a towel, trying to scare Secret away. But Secret trotted over to investigate the towel as Maria backed away, straight towards a trough full of water.

"You horrid thing! Shoo, shoo!" Maria tried to whack Secret across the nose with the towel, missed, and then stumbled back into the trough, sitting down in the water with a huge splash. Secret gazed down at her with a bemused expression before turning round and heading towards Alice.

Everyone was frozen as Maria screamed, pushing her damp hair back from her face. Miraculously her sunglasses remained on top of her head. Finn strode forward, a broad grin on his face, reaching down to pull Maria out of the trough and help her to her feet. No one else had volunteered to help, Alice thought briefly.

"Whoops!" Finn said cheerfully. "At least it's a hot day."

But Maria looked beyond furious. "That…" She pointed a quivering finger at Secret. "That … ghastly creature! He should be destroyed; he's out of control!"

Alice finally had hold of Secret who rubbed his red head up and down her arms with glee, seemingly delighted to be reunited with his

mistress after such a jolly jaunt. Slowly Alice turned back round to face the scene of destruction.

"I'm so sorry. I'll pay for any damage," she said. "Are you OK, Maria?"

"No I'm not!" Maria hissed. "I could have been *killed*!"

"Bit of an exaggeration!" Finn muttered, and Maria shot him a murderous look.

Alice felt totally panicked. Surely they would be sent home now; the fashion team must be high-paying guests and Secret had just ruined hours of work!

"It's OK," Gabby said faintly, looking shell-shocked. "I'm sure we can regroup..."

The fashion team were gathering now, picking up fallen props and tripods and dusting themselves down. Pushing past Finn, a damp and furious Maria jabbed her finger in Alice's face, who shrank back. "What the *hell* are you playing at?" she hissed.

"Don't, Maria," Gabby said sharply as Alice paled. "She didn't do it on purpose."

Maria threw up her hands. "This whole thing has been a disaster," she said angrily. "First the horse freaking out, then that dress getting ruined, now this shoot spoiled by some stupid kid and her stupid pony! What *next*, Gabby?"

"Enough, Maria," Gabby said icily. "These things happen."

"No, they really don't, and they didn't before *you* became editor," Maria hissed. "But you chose this godforsaken place and now we have to deal with dreadful children and their out-of-control ponies!" She turned back to Alice, her eyes flashing. "Well? What do you have to say for yourself?"

"I *am* sorry. I don't know what more to say." Alice, trying to turn Secret round to lead him back to the yard, was close to tears, totally humiliated. Then she heard a familiar voice.

"Don't you dare talk to Alice like that," Finn said to Maria, his tone icy. "No real harm has been done. Don't bother asking for my help again. Come on, Al, I'll help you get Secret back in."

As they walked back down to the yard, the heat shimmering in front of them, Alice glanced at Finn. "Thank you," she mumbled.

Finn smiled, his face full of warmth. "Hey, no problem. What are friends for?" His face darkened for a moment. "I'm quite impressed with Secret, truth be told – the whole fashion thing is ridiculous. They need a taste of the real world!"

Secret walked between them, ambling happily along, and suddenly Alice was transported back to that fateful summer day at the country fair when Secret had run riot over the showground and her world had quite literally collided with Finn's, and life had changed completely.

★

After sitting on her bed for what felt like an age, Alice felt brave enough to creep out into the yard. Surely Maria must have reported the disastrous episode to Mathis and June, and Alice would be in real trouble. But Mathis just gave her a cheery wave and June seemed perfectly happy talking with another district commissioner. Confused, Alice went round to the dining area where Gabby was sitting at her laptop.

"I'm so sorry about earlier," Alice said again, more confidently than she felt. "I'll ring my mum and explain and I'm sure she'll lend me the money to pay you back for the damage caused." *And that'll be my allowance used up for about a hundred years*, she thought sadly. But to her surprise Gabby looked up and smiled.

"Honestly, it's fine," she said distractedly. "Forget about it. We've got loads of those reflector things and we'd got most of the shots we needed.

And Maria *was* fine, just embarrassed. Please don't worry." Then she frowned. "Actually, Alice, there is something. You haven't noticed any of the pony clubbers acting ... unusually, have you?"

"In what way?" Alice asked in surprise.

Gabby ran a hand through her hair. "It's just that someone fiddled around with my laptop over lunch, deleted some important things... I left it by the sofa over there. I shouldn't have left it out, I know."

Alice shook her head, perplexed. She knew that the only guests able to access the communal area were the fashion team and the pony clubbers. *But none of the pony clubbers would want to mess around with Gabby's laptop*, she thought.

Alice had another lesson later that day and Secret performed brilliantly. As she led Secret back to the stables after washing him down she bumped into

Seb, and wished she didn't look quite so hot and bothered.

"Hey!" Seb grinned. "*Just* the girl I wanted to find. I'm showjumping later tonight. I'm going to head down a little early and watch first." Then he gazed right at her. "I'd love it if you could join me, Alice?"

Alice felt her stomach flip. There was something about the way Seb looked at her ... but her thoughts drifted to Finn and his mixed messages – appearing like a knight in shining armour one minute and completely blanking her the next. Alice tried to clear Finn from her head. She wanted to have some fun. An evening watching showjumping with Seb was exactly what she needed!

Chapter 9

The festival was in full swing by the time Alice and Seb headed down to the showjumping. The strum of live music played in the background and the trade stands, selling everything from handmade bridles to Western saddle cloths and showjumping jackets, were busy. A good crowd of people had already started to gather for the evening competition.

In the main arena, the huge showjumps shone, illuminated by the setting pink sun and spotlights, giving the ring a dramatic atmosphere. Grabbing two Cokes, Seb sat down next to Alice, close enough that she could almost feel the warmth of him. He was wearing light breeches and a shirt, ready for his turn in the ring, and his tousled blond hair shone.

"I'll need to head back soon and warm up Clea, but I wanted to spend a little time with you first. You might bring me good luck..." he said in a soft voice.

"Er, thanks," Alice replied. His closeness caught her off guard so she swung the subject back round to horses. "How many classes are you doing?"

"Loads. I'll be doing as much as I can over the festival," Seb explained. Then he looked up and his expression changed. "Uh-oh."

A pretty girl in white breeches came striding up,

her dark hair in a high ponytail. Blanking Alice, she started to speak furiously in French to Seb, a look of fury on her face. Seb held his hands up, replied calmly, and the girl gave a short bitter laugh before turning to Alice.

"Don't get sucked in," she said in accented English, before spinning on her polished boots and stalking off.

"Sorry, Alice." Seb seemed unconcerned. "I won a show last week and she thinks I broke the rules, which I did not."

Hmmm, Alice thought. It didn't exactly sound like an argument over showjumping. From the little she had understood, it sounded like a heated argument between a boyfriend and girlfriend!

When Seb wandered off to get Clea ready, Alice headed over to where the other pony clubbers were sitting.

"Hey, Alice!" Holly waved at her, and Alice

flopped down under the trees.

"Hanging out with gorgeous Seb again?" Holly grinned, taking a huge bite of her burger. "Good for you. I mean, Finn is dreamy, but gosh he's moody!"

Alice knew Holly meant well, but it felt weird comparing the two boys out loud. She knew Finn was moody, but the others would never know about the stuff he had going on behind the scenes, because he wasn't ever going to be the kind of person to open up to people he didn't know well. Mind you, he wasn't exactly opening up to *her* either...

"Oops!" Clapping a hand to her mouth, Holly looked embarrassed as Finn appeared behind them. He'd caught the sun over the last couple of days and looked tanned and relaxed. Alice noticed several girls in the stands swivel round to stare as he passed.

"Finn!" Alice said brightly, hoping he hadn't overheard Holly. "I'm so pleased you're here!"

Settling down as the first class got underway, Finn explained that it was just the fashion team at the chateau that evening. "They were on about the last photos they're taking tomorrow. It's all about a ring. A ring that's worth more than our whole yard." He lay back, placing his hands underneath his dark head, staring up at the crescent moon, which was now hanging in the dusky sky. "It's madness."

The class started, and for the next hour or so the group happily watched the jumping, discussing the good and bad rounds, and it was like it was just Alice and Finn again, chatting away in the horsebox on the way home from a show.

But when Seb cantered in Alice couldn't help but shift forward slightly to get a better look. He jumped a stylish clear, waving at the crowd who clapped as he finished. Then, later, when he won the class, he singled out Alice in the crowd and blew her a kiss. Alice was uncomfortably aware of Finn next to her, who'd gone very still.

"Finn ... I..." Alice began, not really knowing what she was going to say. But just then Seb came racing up to the side of the arena, leaned over the rope and swept Alice up into an embrace. Even though she was distracted by being squashed tightly in his arms, Alice realised that she hadn't seen him yet pat Clea.

"I'm going to find the Rebel Riders," announced Finn.

Finn. Wriggling out of Seb's arms, Alice saw him heading away into the crowds.

"Alice," Seb beamed, seemingly totally unaware of the tension between Alice and Finn. "You brought me luck, like I knew you would! I just won two thousand euros! Let me treat you to a

bite to eat?"

Alice thought about Finn, and how two thousand euros translated to eighteen hundred pounds, more than enough to pay off the yard's debt. Seb was so flippant about that huge amount of money! All of a sudden Alice felt tired, and just wanted to find Finn. She'd seen something in his eyes when he'd left so suddenly. They'd spent so long skirting round the issue of their friendship, never quite telling each other how they felt. She wanted to talk to him, not about the yard and the problems they faced, but about *them*.

"Actually, Seb, sorry," she mumbled. "I'm going to go back to the centre to get an early night. Maybe it's this heat."

Seb scowled at her. He clearly wasn't used to being turned down. But before he could persuade her to stay she was heading up the driveway. The sky suddenly felt unbearably heavy and Alice could feel the beginnings of a headache. She crossed the courtyard and let herself into the cool whitewash of Secret's stable, hoping Finn would be around, but not quite having the energy to go and search for him just yet.

The little gelding was resting a leg, but hearing Alice's footsteps he gave a whicker and crossed sleepily over to see her, burying his nose into the crook of her arm and sighing. Alice bent her head, breathing in his familiar, comforting smell. For some reason she started thinking about Gabby's words from a few days ago, about how it was best to stick with horses. She was right, Alice thought, thinking about Seb and Finn and all her mixed-up feelings. Perhaps it was better just to concentrate on Secret and the competition for now. Then, when she'd hopefully done well and could hand over the prize money to Finn, she'd tell him how she felt. Perhaps then it would finally be the right time.

Chapter 10

The next day Alice was up early to muck out and groom Secret ready for her lesson with Mathis. Finn had already gone out with the Rebel Riders, and Alice had only had time to give him a brief wave as he left the yard.

Secret was in a great mood. As the music from the festival began to drift up to the riding arena he bounded over the jumps and Alice grinned as she pulled him up after their round. She was just glad that they hadn't let the Hilltops branch down during their ridden work. Although Secret had got into one or two scrapes, what with chewing the sign and crashing the photo shoot!

"He's a great pony," Mathis said, smiling. "But I want to see more accuracy from you. It's all very well being able to jump the height, but, believe me, the course builders on Friday will be stretching you all. We'll do some final exercises tomorrow."

Alice nodded. Mathis had told the group more than once that the class would be top standard. She just hoped *she* was up to the standard as well. Accuracy was one thing they struggled with at times, so she needed to work really hard in the next lesson.

Just then Seb strode into the arena and flashed a bright grin at his dad before turning to Alice. "Hey,

you," he said charmingly. "The big day is nearly here!"

Alice nodded. As they neared the end of their stay the competition felt real, and she wanted to do well more than anything else in the world.

"So listen, you heard what my dad said about accuracy. Shall I show you what I would do? Can I ride your pony?" Seb then said to Alice's surprise.

Alice frowned. No one had ever ridden Secret but her, not even Finn.

"Why?" she asked hesitantly.

"If I can feel for myself how he goes, then I can really help you with your final preparations for the competition," Seb suggested. "And it's good for ponies to have another rider every now and again. It would just add another angle, you know?"

Alice thought about this, imagining her and Secret jumping at Hickstead, Alice wearing the cobalt blue jacket she coveted, her feet in the blue stirrups, Secret flying over the jumps like he had wings on his feet. And although she did want to win the prize money for Finn, she wanted to do well for *herself* too. She wanted to be a showjumper, and perhaps Seb could help her achieve her dream. Sure he approached horses differently ... but he was very successful, and clearly knew his stuff.

"OK," she agreed. "He's all warmed up."

Seb grinned. "Great!"

Feeling weirdly apprehensive, Alice climbed down and handed the reins to him. "You don't need to force him, or hold him back. And *no whip*. OK?" she added firmly, and Seb grinned at her.

"It's cool, Alice, you can trust me."

Moments later, Seb was up and on Secret, adjusting the stirrups. Alice immediately got a bad feeling as Seb launched into a trot around the arena. Secret put his ears back, looking perturbed as Seb rode him into an outline, flicking him behind his

saddle with the schooling whip. Alice couldn't tell if the whip had made contact, but she felt anger bubble up inside her. She'd told Seb NOT to use the whip. How dare he ignore her!

"Seb, stop!" Alice shouted, as he pushed Secret into a canter. She started to run across the arena, but Seb aimed Secret at the jump, digging his heels in, his strong hands keeping Secret's neck straight. Secret cleared the jump beautifully, but Seb pulled him back on landing into a strong half-halt, keeping his canter as slow as a walk. Alice knew Secret normally bounded on and she let him, knowing his energy settled after a few jumps. Secret pinned his ears back crossly.

"Seb! Get off!" Alice was really yelling now. But Seb was approaching another jump, Secret's canter controlled, his expression one of annoyance.

"Go on!" Seb flicked him again with the schooling whip, and this time Alice saw it make contact. Clearly having had enough, Secret ran out at the very last second, dropping his shoulder and dumping Seb on to the ground in a heap. Briefly stopping, Secret nipped him on the arm before bounding away.

Seb leapt to his feet, scarlet with anger. "You little—"

But Alice didn't hear what he had called Secret as she rushed towards her pony. He almost crashed into her as she caught him, rubbing his head up and down her arms, covering her shirt in red hair.

"Oh, sweetheart, I'm sorry!" Alice hugged him tightly. She felt awful. Secret had *never* run out, so it was clear to Alice this was his way of saying he didn't like having Seb on his back.

Seb strode across the school, his face dark. "Been a while since I've been thrown," he said with a scowl. "Can you see what I was trying to show you about accuracy, Alice? You need to bring him right

back to you after you jump. OK, I'll get back up and we'll jump it *properly* this time, Caesar."

"His name is *Secret*," Alice said furiously. "And no, you're not getting back on. No way! Never!"

Seb gave her a patronising look. "You're too soft with him! He could be a good pony, but he needs a firm hand."

"I don't think so," Alice said. "I know my pony, and you didn't ride him in the right way. *At all.*"

Before Seb could respond she swung herself up, adjusting her stirrups and patting Secret who visibly relaxed now she was back on board.

Seb shrugged. "Suit yourself. I'm going to go and school my horse. Like, actually *school*. Good luck at the competition – you're going to need it. I'd kiss goodbye to the prize money, if I were you."

He stalked off, leaving Alice and Secret alone.

Picking up her reins, Alice walked Secret around, waiting until he felt relaxed enough, before nudging him into a trot, and then a canter. Secret seemed his normal bouncy self but Alice felt really cross with herself. She'd known Seb had a totally different approach to riding and that his way wasn't right for her or Secret. But she hoped he'd be able to help her to do well, partly for Finn, but mostly because she wanted her and Secret to succeed at something they both loved. It looked like her and Secret had to do it their way.

Secret soared over the jump, and Alice felt much better. Then, looking up over the lavender, she squinted as a familiar rider came into view, heading back to the stables. It was Finn.

"Alice?" There was a frown on Finn's face. "Why was Seb riding Secret?"

Alice rode up to him. "I thought he might have some tips for me. He does really well," she added defensively. She felt guilty about letting Seb ride Secret but he was *her* pony, and so it was really

nothing to do with Finn!

Finn ran a hand through his dusty hair. "Really?" he said coldly. "Did you not notice how he rode? Dad would tear him apart for those heavy hands. Letting him ride Secret was a stupid thing to do."

Alice saw red. "How dare you! I thought it might help to have another opinion and it obviously didn't. It's done now and I don't need *you* making me feel worse!"

Before Finn could reply Seb clattered up on Clea. Suddenly the huge arena felt very small and crowded. The two boys eyed each other warily.

"Finn," Seb said, nodding coolly. "Back from circus training?"

"Just catching up with Alice," Finn replied, his voice equally cold.

"I'm surprised you let her get away with her pony's behaviour," Seb continued, arching an eyebrow. "Great pony ... but spoilt. Maybe if it had better training?"

"The pony is called Secret, and *it's* a he," Finn replied calmly, but his eyes flashed. "And if you knew them at all, you would know how far they've come in a short space of time. Alice doesn't need your input."

Alice felt a rush of anger at the way the boys were discussing her as if she wasn't even there.

"All right Finn, leave it," she said crossly. "And, Seb, thanks for offering to help, but I'm fine as I am. I'll do it *my* way with Secret."

Seb shrugged and gave an insincere smile. "Up to you of course. I like a horse to be obedient. But then I guess *I'm* used to winners."

Chapter 11

With no more activities for the day the pony clubbers were free to come and go, and Lizzie and Beth tried to persuade Alice to go down to the funfair with them.

"Sorry, guys." Alice shook her head. She wasn't feeling very sociable. "I think I'm just going to have a quiet one."

The only place she wanted to be was with Secret,

to have a bit of a think about the busy two days ahead. The festival was at its peak now and the Rebel Riders were giving their big demonstration the next day. With lots of French pony clubbers staying over the night before the class, there was also a dance planned for that evening.

As Alice approached Secret's stable she could see that he had a glint in his eye, one that Alice knew well. He'd been up to mischief. Straight away Alice could tell that he'd been nibbling away at the sign on his door again, and this time he'd taken a small chunk off. Assessing it, Alice groaned. As if the day wasn't bad enough already! Trying to put it back in place, she realised she could lift the sign away from the door now, and doing so left brown stains all over her fingers. She'd have to ask Mathis for some more of the special liquid he'd used, not that it seemed to stop Secret!

"That'll be another thing I have to replace," she

chided her pony as she let herself into the stable, thinking back to the damage he'd caused in the shoot. She was so grateful Gabby had let her off.

Alice sank down into the shavings, and Secret, entirely unconcerned, just nudged her until she couldn't help but laugh, reaching up to play with his forelock. She was so lost in thought that she didn't notice the figure leaning over the stable door and jumped when she heard her name being called.

"Hey, I didn't mean to startle you." It was Celia, leader of the Rebel Riders. As Secret bustled over to say hello, Alice scrambled to her feet, brushing the shavings off her T-shirt, a blush rising in her cheeks. The older girl had such presence that Alice felt quite tongue-tied in her company.

"Listen," Celia continued, "I've found out something really cool. I was talking to one of the guys down at the festival. There's a herd of wild horses quite near here. He said the best way to approach is by horseback, and I have a free afternoon. Want to come, if you have no other plans?"

"Yes please!" Alice gasped – that sounded like a perfect way of spending an afternoon! "I must tell June first."

"Sure," Celia said. "Meet you out here in half an hour?"

"OK!" Alice agreed, letting herself out of the stable. It would be amazing to enjoy some time with Secret, with no pressure. And no boys!

A short while later, Alice was mounted on Secret. Even with just Secret's snaffle bridle and saddle, Alice felt completely overdressed next to Celia, whose beautiful grey horse Domino had just a rope round his strong neck. Hopping into the saddle as Celia swung herself up, Alice smiled. "Ready!"

Once they were climbing up the lavender path and heading to the ridge above the centre, the same one Alice had cantered along with Seb on her first night, Alice felt herself start to relax and lose some of her shyness and the girls were soon chatting away like old friends. Alice started to tell Celia about the showjumping competition.

"I saw you jump in your lesson this morning," Celia smiled. "You both looked great!"

"Thank you." She reached down to pat Secret. "But it hasn't always been like that. Actually, I—" she hesitated for a second— "I got it wrong afterwards. I let Seb ride Secret. I thought it might help with the competition, to have his opinion. And it was totally the worst decision. Secret hated it."

Celia looked thoughtfully at Alice. "We're all human; we make mistakes," she said. "When I watched you jump you were smiling from ear to ear. People can advise all they want but you obviously know Secret best of all. He trusts you, and you need to trust yourself. And always let him be himself; his character is what makes him the pony he is."

They were just the words Alice needed to hear. She smiled gratefully. "Thank you," she said. "That means a lot."

They rode on in contented silence for another mile, climbing a dusty path that led through a lightly wooded area until they reached a clearing and the land levelled out. There were hoof prints everywhere, but it was hard to tell if they belonged to riders on the trail or loose ponies.

"This is where he said they gathered in the afternoons." Celia hopped lightly off Domino's back, before gesturing downwards. Again, to Alice's amazement, the big horse sank down, and had a quick roll before settling into a lying-down

position.

"That's fantastic," Alice said in awe. "I wish I could do that."

"OK," Celia said with a smile. "Let's try!"

Feeling a little embarrassed and half wishing she hadn't said anything, Alice dismounted and removed her saddle. Secret was slightly damp after his climb up the hill and rubbed his head against Alice as if to thank her.

"So," Celia said. "Let's see what Secret can do!"

And with Celia's encouragement Alice stood back and gave Secret the full length of rein. As if he couldn't believe his luck, Secret, who adored nothing more than a good roll, sank to his knees. Using a treat from Celia's pocket, Alice waited until he was finished and about to get up before praising him like he'd just jumped clear at Hickstead and giving him the treat. Secret nosed her hand, nibbling the pony nuts, and then clambered back up, giving himself a shake. Suddenly Alice had a flashback to the time he'd rolled in the arena when she'd been trying to show off in front of Finn, and he'd teased her for ages. She'd been so cross at the time.

"That's it!" Celia grinned. "It takes patience. You can see how I just need to give Domino a little cue, but I would really exaggerate your movement, show Secret what you want him to do, get him to mirror you almost. He's a bright pony – he'll get it."

Alice smiled. "Thanks," she said. "Something cool to practise!"

Then both ponies pricked their ears and Celia nodded to Alice. "Look!" she whispered and Alice gazed in the direction Celia was pointing.

Emerging into the dappled sunlight was the most beautiful grey mare followed by a dark

brown foal. Then another two horses, then another ... until there were ten horses only metres away. Secret was transfixed, uttering a low whinny under his breath. The hairs on the back of Alice's arms stood up as the lead mare lifted her head and stared in their direction, her dark eyes watchful but soft. Alice stood silently, hardly daring to breathe as the foal gambolled and leapt in the long soft grasses, until the herd had crossed the pasture and were out of sight. Secret whinnied once again, and was met with an answering call as the herd disappeared.

"Wow." Celia sounded as awestruck as Alice felt. "That was quite something!"

Alice nodded, unable to think of the words. It had been the most amazing moment, a glimpse into the most magical of worlds.

★

The girls rode back in a relaxed fashion. Alice was

still smiling as she thought about the wild horses. Her mind drifted back to Finn, and she knew he would have loved it as much as she did.

As if reading her thoughts, Celia turned to her. "So, your Finn," she said out of the blue. "He really is an incredible rider. What a shame it looks like he'll have to give up his own team."

Alice was jolted back to the present. "What?" she said, shocked. "Give up the Fillies? I know they have money problems, but the Fillies are going from strength to strength! There's no way he'd give them up!"

Celia bit her lip. "Alice, I'm sorry, I just presumed that you must know." She looked mortified and Alice shook her head. Now she knew why Finn had been so up and down, and why he refused to talk about the Flying Fillies. But to think of giving it all up? Alice tried to make sense of it. He *lived* for his family's display team. What was going on?

They rode back to the centre in silence, Alice's head spinning. She and Finn *had* to talk. But when? And how, when Finn hadn't even told her in the first place?

Chapter 12

Finn was nowhere to be found. He didn't show up for the evening meal or come down to the festival with the rest of the gang. And, after a restless night's sleep, Alice only caught a glimpse of him before she had a lesson with Secret the following morning, the last before the jumping competition.

Secret was brilliant during the lesson. Holding on to Celia's words, Alice finally felt she was the

one who knew her pony best, and it gave her a renewed confidence. They jumped the biggest they'd ever jumped, and Secret remained in control, flying around the course, at one with Alice as they practised the exercises Mathis had set out. It was the most amazing feeling. As she led him back to the dusty paddock afterwards Alice started to believe they had a real shot at the competition.

As she slipped Secret's head collar off Alice remembered what Celia had shown her. Secret was warm, and Alice knew he'd want to roll straight away. She clucked for him to follow her and he did so, rubbing his head on her back. Then, feeling a little silly, Alice checked all around her to make sure no one was watching and bowed towards the ground, scraping the earth like a pony would. Secret also dug with one foot, then another, before flopping down and rolling luxuriously. After he'd rolled a few times on both sides, he paused, and

Alice was ready with a treat. Crouching down, she offered him a mint and he took it, remaining where he was.

"Good boy, clever boy."

Praising him just as Celia had instructed, Alice enjoyed the moment – Secret next to her, the sun warm on her back. Then with a satisfied snort Secret clambered back up and shook the dust from his body before wandering over to pick at the hay. Alice remained on the ground watching him, lost in thought.

★

Later that afternoon, all the pony clubbers went to watch the Rebel Riders in action. Clouds were building and the air felt heavy and oppressive. Despite only wearing a cotton dress Alice was boiling hot.

"We'll have a storm that will clear the air in time for your showjumping tomorrow." Mathis

addressed the pony clubbers with a beaming smile. "Short and sharp, like they are in this region! And then beautiful clear skies to jump."

June clapped her hands and the three Hilltops riders plus half the courtyard turned towards her, such was the booming nature of her voice. "Right, listen up!" She smiled. "I'm leaving you in Mathis's capable hands this evening. I've been given the chance to visit another stables not so far from here, which might be suitable for a trip next year. I'll be back before the end of the night. Be good everyone and enjoy the party!"

★

Gathered with her friends at the ringside, Alice felt the hairs on her arms stand up as Celia galloped in on Domino. She was wearing a scarlet jacket woven with gold thread, and her hair was loose and flowing. Domino's grey mane was plaited with white roses and he looked incredible. The rest of the team galloped in behind her. Their costumes were equally beautiful, from their flowing cloaks and the carvings on the horses' bridles to the silk ribbons and flowers plaited into the flying manes and tails. Everyone gasped and cheered as they thundered across the arena, the blackening sky providing a dramatic backdrop. And then there was Finn. He rode just as well as the rest of the team, throwing himself with ease from his saddle, his head dangerously close to the floor as his pony galloped across the diagonal.

"Wow!" Alice heard Holly exclaim. "I never knew Finn could ride like that!"

Alice felt so proud. But looking at Finn's face as he thundered past, an icy shiver ran down her spine. *Why* was he giving up on the Flying Fillies, something he loved so much?

★

Later on, as the party got under way and music

and laughter filled the air, Alice searched everywhere for Finn. He'd gone back to the stables with the Rebel Riders, and Holly and Beth had bustled Alice back to the courtyard where all the visiting French pony clubbers had gathered. Swept along with them, Alice resolved to find Finn afterwards.

Fairy lights twinkled in the lemon trees and everyone was in a good mood. The pony clubbers and the younger members of the fashion team had started to dance. Alice stood slightly awkwardly with Holly and a few other pony club girls, realising her lack of going to parties over the years meant she had no idea what to do. Should she dance? Should she just stand and try to look cool? Suddenly she found she didn't even know what to do with her hands, and they hung awkwardly by her side, so she shoved them into the pockets of her dress.

"Hi." A familiar voice made her spin round. It was Seb, and the handsome grin was back on his face.

"So, about before," he said, before Alice could say anything. "I'm sorry. I guess we just have different riding styles? Your pony *Secret* is a good jumper. Friends again?"

And he gave her such a sweet smile that Alice couldn't help but laugh. "OK," she said slightly hesitantly. "Friends."

"So." Seb held out his hands. "Friends can dance, right?"

And before Alice could say no Seb pulled her on to the dance floor. He was a good dancer, but Alice self-consciously stepped from side to side. She *really* had no idea how to dance!

"I *am* sorry," Seb repeated. "About Secret. It was wrong of me not to listen to you. You see—" he leaned in a little closer— "I really like you, Alice.

From the very first moment you arrived. I feel bad for upsetting you. Forgive me?"

And as he moved closer still, so Alice could see right into his deep blue eyes, she panicked. This felt all wrong. He wasn't Finn.

"I'm sorry, Seb." She pulled back, ducking under his arm so that she was out of his grasp. "Sorry, I just can't…"

A flash of annoyance crossed Seb's face, but Alice was already walking away, hurrying towards the one creature she knew she could talk to, Secret, before she smacked straight into Finn.

"Finn!" Alice was flustered, her head spinning. "I wanted to see you, earlier, to talk to you…" Her voice faded as Finn gazed at her, an unfamiliar look in his eyes.

"Don't you have somewhere else you need to be?" he said quietly.

Glancing behind her, Alice saw Seb on the dance

floor, his eyes narrowed as he saw Finn and Alice together.

"N-no, not at all," Alice stammered, turning away from Seb. "Actually, it was you I wanted to see—"

"It doesn't matter, Al. See you later." Finn turned to go.

"No!" Alice had had enough. Grabbing his arm, she pulled him towards Secret's stable. "You *have* to tell me what's going on. We're supposed to be friends. And Celia said ... Celia said..." Her voice trailed off.

"Celia said what, Alice?" Finn had crossed his arms.

Alice looked straight at him. "Celia said you were giving up the Fillies."

Finn flinched. "That's right," he replied quietly. "It's the only way."

"But why?" Alice had to know. "Your dad is at

home now and the stables are rebuilt. I thought things were looking good?"

Finn glared at her. "Things are never good for us, though, are they?" he said. "There's always something. Dad might be home, but there's an unpaid bill from last year. Tax stuff. I don't really understand. I just know it's bad, like *really* bad. The Fillies cost a lot to keep going, and Sasha and Dad don't always get on. And Sasha has talked about moving out. She's twenty-three; she has her own life. Dad wants me to carry on, but how, when it just causes everyone stress?"

He sounded so defeated Alice's heart went out to him. But it couldn't be like this. She knew how passionate Finn was about his stunt work, how he came alive when riding. He couldn't just give up!

"Finn Cutler, don't you *dare*!" she cried, making Secret jump. "This *is* your thing! You've totally impressed Celia and the Rebel Riders and,

145

although I know you like riding for Mum it's not really you! *You* always told me never to give up with Secret, and now here you are doing the same thing! The only time I see you truly happy is when you're stunt riding. You have to make it work!"

Finn's eyes flashed dangerously. "I have no choice, unless I rob a bank!" he shouted. "I'm doing this so Dad and Sash don't have to stress any more, so we can just be a normal family."

"You're anything but normal!" Alice said, her voice shrill with emotion. This is your dream, Finn – and you told me it was your mum's dream too, so you need to carry on!"

Emotion swept across Finn's face before he glared at Alice. "You don't know anything about my mum and her dreams," he said, his voice breaking. "Just leave me alone."

And, turning on his heel, Finn disappeared into the darkness.

Chapter 13

Letting herself into Secret's stable and hugging her pony, Alice tried to calm down. She knew just how passionately Finn felt about his stunt riding; she *had* to help him. A beep from her pocket interrupted her thoughts, making both her and Secret jump.

ALICE IT'S MUM. Josephine still texted in capitals, and Alice couldn't help but smile, hearing her mum's bossy voice clearly. *CAN YOU RING ME?*

Alice sank down into the shavings to dial home.

"Hi, Mum, it's me," she said as her mum picked up the phone. "Is everything OK?"

"Oh, everything is fine." Josephine sounded distracted. "How are you? How's Secret? All ready for the class tomorrow?"

"He's fine, Mum. He's being really good. And I hope so."

"Well done, sweetheart."

There was a moment's hesitation before her mum continued. "I just thought I should let you know something," she said softly. "About Finn. I was chatting to Angus today and he told me that it's the two-year anniversary of Finn's mum's death tomorrow." She paused. "Finn insisted he was fine to go to France but Angus is a bit worried. Anyway, I thought I'd let you know, given how

close you are. You can keep a bit of an eye on him, make sure he's OK."

Alice felt herself go hot and cold. She couldn't have picked a worse time to argue with Finn. And she'd mentioned his mum! No wonder he'd freaked out.

"Alice?" her mum said. "Are you still there?"

"Sorry, yes." Alice shook herself back into the present, and tried to keep her voice steady. "Thanks for letting me know. I'll look out for him. Love you, Mum."

"Love you, Alice. Good luck tomorrow – I know you'll both do well!" And as her mum rang off Alice knew she needed to find Finn and let him know she was there for him.

Letting herself out of the stable, Alice scanned the yard. Finn couldn't have gone far. She decided to try the area by the lavender fields where the Rebel Riders practised. That's where he'd spent most of the week after all. Alice had just taken a deep breath and broken into a run when a loud screech filled the air.

★

Changing direction and rushing back to the courtyard, Alice took in the scene in front of her. The music had stopped, and everyone had gathered around Maria, who was standing with her hands on her hips apparently furious. Gabby appeared looking pale.

Alice nudged Holly. "What's going on?"

"Something is missing – a ring, I think," Holly whispered back. "Maria, that mean lady, thinks someone stole it."

Alice remembered the ring that Finn had mentioned, and how he'd told her it was worth more than the value of the yard.

"I knew something like this would happen!" Maria hissed. Then she turned furiously to Gabby.

"This is your fault!" she cried. "You left the safe open!"

Gabby looked distraught. "Enough, Maria!" she said quietly. "Let me think! I remember putting the ring in the safe… Let's think about what we were all doing this afternoon… We need to search our bags and the equipment boxes…"

"Look," Mathis said in a reasonable voice, "I'm sure the ring has just been misplaced. I can't imagine that anyone here would steal such an item. Let's gather up everyone staying here and we can ask people if they've seen the ring or spotted anything unusual."

In no time at all the UK pony clubbers and the Rebel Riders, the only two groups with access to the living quarters, were rounded up in front of the big house. Everyone, that is, but Finn.

Mathis frowned as he made a head count. "One missing. Alice, have you seen Finn?"

Alice shook her head. "No, I was with him, but then he headed off somewhere."

"We need to talk to everyone together," Mathis said, opening the door to the house. "Finn?" he called out, but there was no answer.

"Where is he?" Sam whispered to Alice, and she shook her head, noticing that the others were all looking at her too.

"I don't know," she replied quietly.

"Actually, Dad?" Seb pulled Mathis aside, glancing at Alice as he spoke to him quietly. Mathis frowned.

Suddenly Alice's spine was icy, and a sickening feeling pitted in her stomach. There was something in Seb's expression that told her he was talking about Finn, and he wasn't saying anything good.

"I think we call the dance off now," Mathis announced, looking serious. "We need to sort all this out."

As Mathis turned his attention to the panicked fashion team, Alice pulled Seb aside. "What did you say to your dad?" she asked quietly.

Seb frowned at her. All the warmth had gone from his blue eyes. "I just said that my dad should probably talk to Finn first," he said coldly. "After all, didn't you tell me he had financial problems?"

Alice felt herself flush right to her ears. "That's not fair!" she hissed. "Finn wouldn't take anything – I know he wouldn't! He's the most honest and trustworthy person I know."

Seb just raised an eyebrow at her. "You *really* know that, do you?" he replied. "You barely see him. He spends all his time in his room or with those Rebel Riders. And he seems to have it in for the magazine team…Who knows what he's been up to?"

Alice glared at Seb. "What have you got against Finn? There are loads of people here – anyone could have taken, or misplaced, the ring."

Seb gave her a pitying look as he stalked off. "Oh, Alice. You're only seeing what you want to see…"

Feeling sick, Alice ran back to Secret's stable, needing to gather her thoughts. Alice noticed he'd been nibbling even more off his box sign. She groaned. She'd have to deal with that later. Then Alice jumped as Celia padded past with several bridles hanging from her arm.

"Alice," Celia said kindly, "are you OK?"

"I don't know…" Alice whispered. "I need to find Finn."

Celia looked at her. "You know," she said softly, "he talked about you a lot when we were riding. I know he didn't tell you everything that was going on back home, but I think it's because he's proud. It's you who means the most to him."

As Celia walked on, Alice headed back outside,

determined to find Finn. She wanted to make sure no more suspicion was cast against him, but more importantly she wanted to tell him she knew about the significance of the date. And that she was there for him.

Despite the party being over, everyone was still gathered in the courtyard, the air humming with the buzz of conversation. Gabby and Maria were standing next to each other.

"Look, let's all have a good search through our rooms and through all the equipment, then if we still can't find it, let's call in the police and deal with this properly," Gabby said.

Alice noticed a strange smug smile flit across Maria's face.

"Good idea," she snapped. "Let's start right away. But what about the kid that's missing? That boy, Finn? Perhaps he has something to do with it? After all, he *hates* us after the trouble with that horrid red pony at the shoot the other day."

Alice felt panic wash over her like a cold shower. She had to find Finn, and soon…

Chapter 14

"Is it true?" Alice jumped as Holly came rushing up to her an hour later in the communal area. No one seemed to have gone to bed. Alice had walked the whole of the site several times looking for Finn, but with no luck. He seemed to have totally disappeared.

"Is what true?" Alice frowned at her friend.

"Finn!" Holly said in a shocked voice. "I mean,

he seems troubled, but I never imagined he was a thief! Maria has been saying he had something against the fashion team. And Seb said that the ring has been stolen, that Finn needed money and might try to sell..." Her voice trailed off as Alice glared at her.

"No, Holly," she snapped. "He didn't steal it. And whatever Seb or Maria say, it's not true!"

"I heard he got in with the fashion team just to see what he could steal!" Lizzie added cattily.

Sam, hovering nearby, responded crossly. "That's not fair. They asked *him* to help, didn't they, Alice?" And Alice nodded, grateful to kind Sam.

"He never joined in with us lot, did he, though?" Dai, one of the boys from the Welsh club, piped up.

"Listen!" Alice yelled. "Whoever has been stealing, it's not Finn! He's not here to defend himself so he's an easy target!"

Clearly surprised by her outburst, everyone started to drift away, muttering quietly to themselves, and Alice went out to the stable yard. Thunder rumbled in the distance as raindrops began to fall. One of the French pony clubbers had said a big storm was rolling through the region and had already flooded some land further south.

Heading to Secret's stable, Alice jumped as Maria strode past, pausing at the stable door and glaring at her so furiously that Alice shrank back. She didn't dare ask Maria what she was doing in the stable yard in the rain.

Leaving the shelter of the yard and climbing up the hill, the raindrops heavy and warm, Alice scanned the open horizon. The festival site was shut up and it was silent at the top of the ridge apart from the soft pat of rain on the dust.

"Oh, Finn," Alice said aloud. "Where *are* you?"

★

There was little point in going to bed. Instead Alice flopped down in Secret's stable, determined she'd keep watch as the rain continued to fall. But as her eyelids grew heavier and Secret fell asleep resting one leg Alice drifted off, totally exhausted.

She awoke with a start a few hours later as pink tendrils of early-morning light crept on to the horizon. The rain had stopped, but the air was still heavy. It felt like the sky was about to fall in, great swathes of scarlet reflecting on the whitewashed stables as the storm rolled in. Alice glanced at her watch. It was barely five a.m. The day of the competition! She decided she'd resume her search for Finn after changing into shorts and sorting Secret out.

To her surprise she wasn't the only one in the stables when she returned a few minutes later. Clea was swishing her tail as Seb swung himself up in the saddle. He glared at Alice.

"What are you doing out so early?" Alice asked.

Seb gave her a disparaging look. "You pony clubbers might be happy with amateur jumping competitions," he said scornfully. "But later I'll be jumping against the best. So I'm practising now, before you all come out on your little ponies."

Alice glanced at the sky. "But the storm seems to be closing in."

Seb shook his head. "I know the area," he sneered. "I think *I'll* be OK. Let's hope circus boy makes his way back soon! He has some explaining to do."

Alice felt a flush of anger. "That's not fair!" she hissed. "He didn't take the ring."

Seb just raised an eyebrow. "You keep believing that, Alice." Then he took Clea out to the arena and was soon soaring over the big showjumps.

Alice went back to Secret to muck out and feed him. Moments later Secret gave a little whicker as Clea and Seb clattered past, heading down the drive.

"Seb, are you *sure* you should be riding out?" Alice called, but her words were lost in the strong breeze that had whipped up again, swirling the shavings off her fork and dancing around the cobbles as the trees rustled and whispered. A low rumble of thunder echoed on the horizon.

The air felt almost electric and the ponies shuffled in the stables as if sensing the atmosphere. The first drops of heavy hot rain started to fall, splashing on the yard faster and faster until the sky looked as though someone had turned a shower on. Seb had to be mad riding in this, Alice thought, expecting to see him turning back into the yard at any minute. But there was no sign of him, and from the shelter of Secret's stable Alice watched as rivulets of water started to wash through the yard, the raindrops on the tiles above almost deafening.

Sticking her hand out of the door, the force of the rain stung her palm. It was like nothing she'd ever seen.

Alice thought back to their arrival. June had said something about the dip at the start of the drive, and how it became a ford if there was heavy rain. *How fast does a flash flood happen?* Alice thought, desperately trying to remember her geography lessons. Feeling panic grip her, she realised she had to go and look for Finn again. He could be trapped or hurt somewhere, or worse. Then Secret looked up sharply as Alice heard the scrabble of hooves on the cobbles. Clea lurched into sight, her reins broken and her saddle to one side.

Leaping forward, Alice grabbed the big warmblood's trailing reins, quickly pulling her saddle off and leading her into her stable. The horse seemed fine, but where was Seb?

Weighing up her options, and realising there was

no time to waste, Alice quickly fastened Secret's head collar on, grabbed her skullcap and led him out.

She vaulted on to him, allowing herself a tiny moment of pride that she'd managed to do so. "Come on, boy, let's go."

Nudging Secret with her heels, she winced as they rode into the deluge. The rain was warm but stung her eyes and bare arms and soaked through her clothes in seconds. There was no sign of Mathis or anyone else connected to the horses.

Seb is probably on his way up the drive, she thought. *Wet, but OK.* She'd find him in just a minute. But as she rode down the drive, the streams cutting great swathes through the once dusty road, and the sound of water rushing in her ears, there was no sign of him. Heavy rain was still falling and Secret's red mane was plastered to his strong neck. His ears were flat against his head, face

tucked into his chest, but still he powered forward, listening to Alice. She pushed him into a trot, Secret's strides eating up the ground.

At first Alice couldn't make anything out in the bubbling, swirling ford that marked the start of the long drive. The trickle of water that they had driven through on the day of their arrival was now a wide churning rush of murky water, and Alice wondered if it was being fed from a collapsed dam somewhere upstream. Then she gave a cry of horror. Seb was submerged in the deep water, his brown arms clinging to a spindly-looking sapling that hung over the water. Seeing Alice, he gave a panicked wail.

"Help me!"

Chapter 15

For what seemed like forever Alice stared at Seb, her brain frozen. Then she shook herself. She had to do something. Gingerly she led Secret towards the water's edge.

"Help me," Seb cried again. "I've done something to my leg and the current is too strong." Then he gave a panicked shout and Alice watched in horror as he jerked violently. "The branch is snapping!"

"Don't panic!" Alice shouted, although she knew he'd be swept away if the branch broke. All kinds of debris was rushing through the muddy water so she knew he would struggle to swim through it. Then she thought about something she'd watched on the news once, about the rescue of a dog from a river. Four men had made a human chain and pulled the dog to safety. But it was just Alice … and Secret.

Alice looked at her little gelding, an idea starting to form. Holding on to his head collar, she stretched out her arms, estimating their reach, before unclipping Secret's lead rope.

"Seb," she called urgently. "I'm going to throw the lead rope to you. Try to catch it. Come on, Secret!"

Alice clung on tightly to Secret's head collar as she tentatively moved forward into the water. The current swirled around her ankles and knees until it reached her waist and she didn't dare go any further in. Taking a deep breath, Alice threw the lead rope, and cursed as it landed with a splash behind Seb. She pulled it back and gasped as the branch sagged even further. She *had* to get this right. She threw again, and this time the rope landed with perfect precision on Seb's shoulder, just as the branch gave way with an almighty crack, plunging into the churning water. For one awful second Alice thought Seb had also been washed away, but the sudden weight on her right arm told her he'd got hold of the rope.

"OK, Secret," Alice said. "Back up, back up!"

Secret snorted, taking the weight of both Seb and Alice, and took a couple of steps back. One step back, then another, and Alice's yard boots were slipping and sliding in the muddy ground. Just another and Seb would be in reach of the bank.

Then Alice's feet slipped, and she fell heavily

on to her hip. Secret spooked sideways as the sudden movement frightened him. Only years of falling off ponies and grimly hanging on to reins helped Alice. She still had hold of Secret's head collar *and* the lead rope. The rope was burning as it pulled through her hand, but she held on as Secret continued to back away. After what felt like an age Seb was finally dragged from the water, falling back as he collapsed on the bank, spluttering and gasping, and Alice finally let go of Secret.

For a few seconds they were silent, trying to get their breath back before Alice staggered to her feet, then Secret whickered and wheeled back to her. Pressing her forehead against his, she thanked him silently.

Kneeling beside Seb, Alice saw that his breeches were torn and covered in blood, his knee badly swollen. He was freezing cold and shivering violently.

"It's OK, Seb, you're safe now," she said, trying to sound calm despite her heart hammering against her chest. "What happened?"

"Clea spooked." Seb's tanned face was horribly pale. "Bolted and then threw me on the edge of the ford, and I caught my knee on that—" he pointed to a gnarled-looking tree stump, and Alice winced— "I was pulled in, but I managed to hold on to the branch."

"We need to get help." Pulling her phone from her pocket, Alice groaned in frustration. It was soaking wet and wouldn't turn on.

Alice knew she needed to get Seb back up to the centre, and fast. For a second she felt very alone. But she shook herself, realising it was down to her to help him. And she wasn't really alone. She had Secret.

"Seb, listen," she said. "You're going to have to ride back to the chateau."

Seb stared at her. "Alice," he said with a trace of his former arrogance, "have you *seen* my leg?"

"Yes, I have," Alice said with a frown, "but I'm going to give something a try." Turning away from him, she patted Secret. "Right," she said. "This is a big thing, but please try, for me."

And then, exactly as Celia had showed her, Alice stood back from Secret. She gestured towards the ground, bowing and scraping the ground, trying to encourage her pony to roll.

"What *are* you doing?" Seb said impatiently.

"Trying to help you!" Alice said between gritted teeth. "Try to drag yourself over here using your good leg and get ready to climb!"

Seb staggered slowly to his feet and hobbled over.

Alice turned back to Secret. He definitely wanted to roll, Alice could tell. As he started to sink Alice praised him, and just hoped he'd stay down long enough for Seb to clamber on. She had a packet of mints in her pocket. They had disintegrated in the water, but there was enough left for her to smear the minty paste on to her hand for Secret to lick off.

Helped by Alice and half using his own strength, Seb hauled his good leg over Secret, giving a sharp gasp of pain as his bad knee took his weight for a second. Startled, Secret lurched to his feet. Gripping on to his red mane, Seb managed to stay on, and Alice gave a deep sigh of relief as Secret rolled his eyes at her.

"Well done, boy." She gave his forehead a stroke.

Side by side Alice and Secret walked slowly back up the drive towards the centre. The rain had finally stopped, and everything seemed to sparkle. The whole rescue started to feel like a bit of a dream.

"Alice!"

Appearing from a trail that led off from the drive

was Finn. Alice didn't think she'd ever felt so relieved. Today was the second-year anniversary of his mum's death, and she still wanted desperately to tell Finn that she knew, and that she was there for him. But she couldn't say anything, not in front of Seb.

"Where have you been?" she cried instead. "I've been searching for you all night!"

"I just went for a walk that went on and on," Finn said, his eyes widening as he looked at Seb slumped on Secret's back. "When the storm came I found a barn to shelter in. What happened?"

Alice realised that she, Seb and Secret made quite a strange sight! Suddenly Alice's legs felt weak, the adrenalin finally wearing off. "Walk with us," she said wearily. "And I'll explain on the way back."

★

They were met by Mathis in the yard, who had just

arrived to start the morning routine.

"Sebastian!" Mathis rushed up to his son, and with another groom's help managed to get him off Secret's back. Deathly pale and in pain, it was clear Seb needed urgent medical attention.

Mathis put Seb's arm round his shoulder and escorted him towards the house, ringing for an ambulance as he did so. Then, when the call was finished, he looked at Finn, and Alice couldn't read his expression.

"We need to talk, Finn, when I've made sure my son is OK."

Finn watched Mathis hurry away and then turned to Alice. "What did he mean?" He sounded totally confused and Alice took a deep breath.

"The fashion team have had a valuable piece of jewellery go missing, a ring, and, um, well, they are just eliminating possibilities, and you weren't here... I'm sure it's nothing." She blustered over

her words. She felt terrible, partly blaming herself for telling Seb about Finn's money troubles.

There was a minute or two of silence as Finn let the words sink in.

"And they think I've taken it?" he asked Alice, his dark eyes unreadable.

Alice couldn't do anything else other than nod.

Chapter 16

Finn helped Alice put Secret away, checking his legs over and sponging off the worst of the mud. He was absolutely fine and happy to turn his full attention to his hay net.

Just then a police car pulled up, and Mathis came to the door to meet them. Alice was sure he glanced over at her and Finn.

"Who called the police?" Maria suddenly

appeared along with Gabby, looking alarmed.

Gabby frowned. "Mathis did. If someone *did* take the ring, we need to find out who, and fast. You know how much it's worth, Maria."

"Well, if you hadn't been so careless in the first place…" Maria snapped, glaring at Finn and Alice.

"I didn't take the ring," Finn replied in a level tone. "I don't know why you would think that."

Gabby placed a hand briefly on Finn's arm. "Don't worry," she said quietly as the policeman came over with Mathis. "They'll talk to everyone; it isn't just you."

"But perhaps we can talk with you first?" The policeman directed Finn towards the living area. "It won't take long."

Finn followed Mathis and the policeman, glancing back at Alice. She shook her head, hoping he'd hear her thoughts somehow and know that she was going to try to help him. Finn didn't deserve this, she thought angrily. Today of all days.

Secret nudged her and she reached up to stroke his mane. Then he leaned over the door and began chewing on his damaged box sign.

"Not now, Secret!" Alice cried in an irritated voice as she tried to move his muzzle away. "I've enough to think about without you destroying your stable!" Defiantly Secret looked right at her and pulled hard on the sign, lifting it away from the door altogether. The movement caused something shiny to fall out from behind the sign and land on the cobbles. Alice's heart beat faster as she bent to pick it up, examining a ring as its huge cluster of diamonds shone in the morning sunlight.

"Secret," she said slowly, turning to her little red gelding in disbelief, "what *is* this doing here?"

Thinking hard, Alice turned the ring over in her hand. Someone must have put the ring there … but who? And why? As she stared hard at the

glittering ring she noticed that despite the heavy rain *and* being soaked in the ford her index fingers and thumbs were still stained from the no-chew lotion slathered on the sign. The ring had to have been put behind the sign deliberately … and whoever had put it there would also have stains on their hands.

Her heart in her mouth, Alice ran over to the communal area where the police were sitting with Finn. Maria and Gabby were in a huddle away from the table with some other members of the fashion team. Finn was doing his best to answer the questions.

"You don't know where you were last night?" The policeman was making notes as Finn sat in front of him.

"I don't know the area," Finn said quietly. "I just kept walking."

"And what *time* was this?"

"I don't know," Finn mumbled. "I don't wear a watch."

The policeman shrugged. "OK, well, thank you, we'll perhaps have some more questions later. Did you notice anything unusual before you left on your walk?"

Finn shook his head. "No, nothing."

"Um … sorry to interrupt."

Alice blushed as everyone turned to stare at her as she held the ring in front of her. "I found this."

Quick as a flash Maria and Gabby jumped up. Alice noticed Maria had turned very pale.

"Where did you find that?" she hissed.

"It was tucked behind the sign on Secret's stable. Actually, it was Secret who found it," Alice said, keeping her voice steady. "Is it the missing ring?"

"Yes, that's it." Gabby looked extremely relieved but very serious as the policeman examined the ring. "But how did it get there?"

"Yes, how?" Maria repeated. "What was it doing in *your* stable?" She looked pointedly behind Alice at Finn, and following her gaze, Alice felt a rush of anger.

"It wasn't Finn!" she said. "Why on earth would Finn take the ring and then hide it there?"

"Ha," Maria snorted. "You two are in on it together, I'm sure!"

Gabby frowned. "Maria, stop – there's no evidence against Finn or Alice," she said. "Now we know the ring was hidden in the stables, we can check the footage from the CCTV cameras."

Alice noticed Maria grow even paler, and as she pushed her sunglasses up her head in a haughty manner, her hand trembled.

Alice blinked. As she fiddled with her sunglasses she saw that Maria's perfectly manicured hand had a large brown smudge near the fingertips. Alice held her own hands in front of her, examining the stain from the no-chew lotion.

"Maria," Alice asked quietly, "what made that mark on your hand?"

Maria glared at Alice. "I have no idea what you are talking about," she hissed, quickly crossing her arms.

Alice held up her own hands. "Look," she said slowly. "These marks are from the sign where the ring was found. They're caused by the lotion that we put on the sign to stop Secret chewing it. I think that whoever took the ring and hid it behind the sign will also have this stain on their hands."

Alice noticed a flicker of panic cross Maria's face as Gabby turned towards her, a questioning look on her face.

"Show me your hands, Maria," she said firmly, her voice authoritative. Reluctantly Maria held out her hands in front of her. There was no mistaking the marks.

She tried to laugh. "Don't be absurd! It's all so dirty around here... You have no proof..." But it was clear she was panicking.

"*You* put the ring there," Alice burst out angrily. "But *why*?"

And then, to the shock of everyone in the room, Maria snapped.

"It wasn't meant to happen like this, Gabby," she screeched. "I had to make people realise that things *always* go wrong when you're in charge. You're too soft, letting the kids off when the ponies ruined things, inviting complete strangers to help with the photo shoots. And so careless! I just thought if the ring went missing on your watch then other people would see what is so obvious. That you should *never* have got the job of editor."

"I-I don't understand!" Gabby looked horrified. "*You* took the ring from the safe?"

"You left it open! I was going to put it back when

I'd given you a scare and taught you a lesson," Maria said defiantly. "I *didn't* steal it!"

"And you told everyone you thought it was *Finn* in order to teach Gabby a lesson?!" Alice could feel herself boiling with anger at the unfairness of it all.

"I wasn't trying to frame him! He did that to himself when he went missing. I was always going to put the ring back!" Maria hissed.

"Hello, what's going on?" June burst through the door, an anxious look on her face. Alice suddenly realised in all the drama last night that June had never made it back to the centre.

"The road was blocked by the flood," June continued. "I've had the most awful journey. Now, what's happened? What are the police doing here?"

As June caught up on what had happened Alice's adrenalin started to wear off again and she felt exhausted. She gave a start as Finn slipped his hand into hers.

"Thank you," he whispered.

"Finn, I…" She spoke softly so only he could hear. "I know what day it is today. Your mum … I just want to say I'm sorry, and I'm here for you."

Finn squeezed her hand. "I know," he said quietly. "We'll talk later. But first, you've got a showjumping competition!"

Chapter 17

Just a few minutes later, Alice was back in the yard. She could hardly believe the events of the past few hours. First rescuing Seb, then proving Finn hadn't stolen the ring – it was all so extraordinary! She needed time to digest it all, but the big competition was finally here and Alice knew she had to put the events of the night behind her for now and do well. For herself, for Finn and for her beloved pony.

She gave Secret an extra good brush, before changing into her cream jodhpurs and navy jacket, her hands shaking slightly as she tied her stock. Scooping her pale hair into a bun, and fastening her velvet hat, she took a deep breath. There was always something to jump for – a place in the team, success at an area event, a red rosette – but jumping for Finn and the Flying Fillies today seemed the most important reason of all. She was exhausted, but she had to keep going. For just a few hours more! Secret danced a little as Alice led him from the stable and swung herself up into the saddle.

"Alice, are you OK?" Holly joined her on Minstrel as they set off down the drive. "We heard that you rescued Seb – you're amazing! And everyone is saying that *Maria* had something to do with the missing ring?"

Alice nodded, remembering Holly's horrible comments about Finn, and Holly paused.

★

★
★

"Look," she continued. "We're all really sorry about what we said about Finn. Seb and Maria were saying stuff and—"

"It's fine," Alice said shortly. "But it's Finn who you really need to apologise to."

"You're right." Holly nodded. "We'll do that."

Just then June came jogging over. "Alice," she said in a kind voice. "You brave girl. You must be so tired; are you sure you still want to jump?"

It hadn't even occurred to Alice *not* to jump! She nodded her head. "I'm absolutely sure," she said firmly, patting Secret. "We're ready. I can catch up on sleep later."

"OK." June was back in district commissioner mode. "Well, I had a look at the course on the way back," she said briskly. "It's up to height, no doubt about it."

As Alice and Secret neared the arena a few minutes later she could see what June meant.

Mathis had been right. The jumps were enormous, huge spreads seeming to stretch as wide as the ocean and uprights that felt as high as tower blocks.

"Yikes!" Holly gulped, patting her pony. "I think Minstrel and I will just jump the easy ones, keep it safe."

But Alice was already planning her route, working out which ones she needed to jump to gain the maximum score. She'd never felt prouder of Secret and more convinced of their special bond. This was her big chance, and she was going to go for it!

★

Alice wasn't feeling *quite* so confident after walking the course. The top scoring jumps were not only big but technical as well. She couldn't just cling on and hope for the best if Secret got out of control. The strides had to be ridden accurately, the corners taken with pinpoint precision. And the last fence on the course – the joker fence – was bigger than anything Alice had ever jumped, with a hairpin corner leading up to it. This, the highest-scoring jump on the course, had to be ridden perfectly.

"Just do your best," June said, giving Secret a pat. "And enjoy it."

Gathering up her reins and trying to smile, Alice searched the crowd for Finn. She hoped he'd managed to get to the festival in time. But there was no time to worry about it. Alice trotted into the arena, steadying Secret, who snorted at the flags. She'd planned her route carefully, trusting her own judgement, and hoping to play on Secret's strengths, his astonishing turns of speed and nimble feet. But the jumps were huge! Then the bell rang, and Alice felt the nerves grip her stomach as she turned into the first fence, a green and white upright.

"Steady, steady…" Alice whispered under her breath.

The stands were silent as Secret soared the first, and then the second and third and the double, following the course she'd planned. Clear so far. As each jump disappeared under Secret's neat hooves Alice started to relax, to believe. Secret felt brilliant, in perfect sync. Maybe they *could* do this, but she had to keep her focus.

On round the corner and to the hanging gate. It was enormous. For just a split second Secret felt a little unsure and Alice knew it was up to her to guide him. Sitting as quietly as she could in the saddle, keeping her contact light, she encouraged him into the jump, feeling him lift and soar. Then on to the next, and the next, and Alice could tell Secret was trying his absolute best in a class that was well above his comfort level. His willingness to do well for her was overriding his inexperience;

191

he was trying so hard. Nearly there, still clear, but she had to decide now what she was going to do. If she jumped the joker and got it wrong, they'd lose all their points, but more importantly Secret might lose his confidence.

Third to last, and Secret, his ears flicking back and forth, slightly misjudged his take-off and there was a gasp from the crowd as Alice clung on to his mane, feeling airborne for what felt like minutes. Although he had the scope, his – and Alice's – inexperience was starting to show with the stridings. The pole rolled in the cups, but miraculously stayed up.

They turned down to the penultimate fence, an easier upright, and Secret flicked an ear back. They had just ten seconds left to jump, enough time to try the joker ... but should they go for it?

"I'm doing my best. I'll try, for you!" Secret seemed to say as he jumped the penultimate fence, and

Alice's mind was suddenly clear. Instead of turning the sharp corner down to the joker, she swung a wide right and cantered around the arena, slowing him to a bouncy trot and patting him over and over. Secret gave a little leap of joy, as if elated by his clear round. Alice knew she'd done the right thing. The joker was a step too far for them both – for now at least!

"Good round, Alice!" June Darby was beaming happily as Alice rode out. "What a great score!"

Then Seb appeared and Alice gave a start. He was on crutches and looked very pale.

"Alice," he said. "Thanks for, you know, saving me. And thank you, Secret."

He reached out to pat the little roan who eyed him suspiciously.

"Really, it's fine." Alice didn't quite know what to say.

"What happened there, though? You could have

jumped the joker! You were flying!"

"I didn't want to risk it." Alice felt totally at ease as she replied to Seb, knowing in her heart that she'd made the right choice.

"*I* would have risked it," Seb replied airily and Alice looked straight at him.

"Then I guess that's the difference between you and me," she said firmly, turning away from him as she saw Finn approach. Her heart leapt but then fell again. Alice knew she'd jumped brilliantly, but she'd surely missed out on the prize money, and she'd so wanted to help Finn.

Finn smiled. "Alice, that was amazing!"

There was a pause, and before Alice could say anything else he took her hand again.

"And thank you. For everything!" His voice quietened. "I thought I was doing OK, but it's all been getting to me since we've been here. It was Gabby that made me think of Mum. I mean, I think

of her every day, but Gabby really reminded me of her."

Alice's tummy jolted as she remembered how Gabby had seemed familiar. She thought about the photo in Finn's kitchen, of Finn's mum riding side-saddle and laughing, so carefree and beautiful.

"Mum would have known what to do with everything that's going on," he continued. "Dad and I are too alike; we run away or get angry. But I want that to change. Since meeting you, and Secret, and riding for your mum, I guess it's the most secure I've felt in ages, and I'm as scared of losing all that as I am about the Flying Fillies."

And for a second he looked so young and totally vulnerable.

"But you won't!" Alice cried. "Whatever happens when you get back Mum will still want you to ride for her, and I'll…" She blushed, wondering how to say it. "I'll always be your friend."

Suddenly, she had an idea. She wanted them to get away from the hustle and bustle of the competition. Alice had been one of the first to jump, and with at least fifty pony clubbers entered, the class would go on for hours yet. She knew the perfect place to take Finn.

"Finn?" she asked hesitantly, thinking of all the times he'd refused to come out with her during the week. "Do you want to go riding with me?"

Finn smiled at her. "I can't think of anything I'd like to do more."

Chapter 18

Celia lent Finn one of the Rebel Riders' ponies, and soon Alice and Finn were clattering out of the yard and on to the path up towards the lavender fields that were now completely dry, having been deluged just a few hours earlier. There were a few people heading back to the stables from the showjumping, either on foot or by pony.

Alice had to look twice as Seb limped up on

crutches, his arm encircling the same pretty girl from the evening showjumping, the one who'd argued furiously with him. Judging by the way she was cuddled up to him now, whispering in his ear, it looked like he'd been forgiven. Looking up as Finn and Alice approached, Seb at least had the good grace to look embarrassed.

"Oh, hey, Alice, Finn. This is Sylvie, um, my girlfriend," Seb said, and Alice smiled to herself. *Of course* Seb had a girlfriend. She realised she didn't mind at all.

"Pleased to meet you," she said politely. "Hope you feel better soon, Seb."

"Oh, Seb will be back to his winning ways soon," Sylvie purred.

Alice smiled. "I'm sure he will. Have a good rest of the day!" she said, nudging Secret on.

Secret gave Seb a sideways look, his ears flicking backwards. At least her pony was a good judge of

character, Alice thought wryly.

Finn shot her a glance as they rode past. "OK?" he said once they were safely out of earshot.

"Perfect," Alice said, and she meant it.

★

They rode on, following the track up through a forest, which then opened up into meadow, and Alice tried to remember various landmarks from her afternoon with Celia. The land stretched out before her, a vibrant mix of purple and green and sandy yellow. It was brilliant being back with Finn, riding out, just the two of them, and they could have been at home, riding on the downs that lay above Park Farm. Then suddenly they were in the clearing. Alice held her breath. Were they going to be lucky a second time?

"What are we waiting for?" Finn whispered next to her, and Alice smiled at him.

"Let's just stay here."

★
★
199
★

And as she gazed around her, hoping and waiting, Alice remembered what she'd been going to explain to Finn, right after she'd left Seb on the dance floor. There was still so much unsaid.

As if reading her thoughts, Finn turned to her. "Are you sure you're not upset over Seb?" he said in a low voice.

"Not at all," Alice whispered.

"It's just that..." Finn looked like he was struggling for the right words. "He really seemed into you, and I guess I thought I couldn't compete."

Alice stared at him. "What?" she said quietly. "You were jealous of Seb?"

Finn shrugged. "Yes, I was."

Alice blinked. Finn, jealous? "But I thought you were pushing me away!"

"I did," Finn said. "Because I knew as soon as I told you about the Flying Fillies it would become real. And I wasn't ready for that. But I don't want

to push you away any more. I want you to be part of my life, more than you are already. Since my mum died it's been the worst of times, but it's been the best of times too. Whatever happens at home, I've got you, and Secret. In fact," he said with a chuckle, "I have Secret to thank for a lot of stuff, really."

Alice smiled, thinking of how Secret had brought her and Finn together all those months ago.

Then, moving his pony closer, Finn took Alice's hand, and she felt a shiver run through her whole body as he leaned in, closer and closer, until their faces were only millimetres apart. Alice's mind was going at a million miles an hour. She half closed her eyes and then...

"Look!" A movement had caught her eye, and both ponies raised their heads as the mare Alice had seen before appeared with her foal at foot, followed by another and another, until a whole herd of wild horses came into view.

Drawing back, Finn smiled, and they watched silently as the horses drifted across the meadow. They started to graze or roll luxuriously, before they wheeled round and cantered away, their tails streaming behind them.

"Wow," Finn whispered. "Thank you." Then he paused for a minute, before his voice cracked with emotion. "I can't think of a more perfect way to spend today."

★

They rode back in contented silence, but Alice's brain was in overdrive. That had been the most amazing moment ... but Finn had been about to kiss her, and she'd been distracted by the horses! She had no idea how to even address that. But soon her thoughts were interrupted by Holly running towards her, face flushed, eyes sparkling.

"Alice!" she yelled in an excited voice. "Where

have you been?" Then without waiting for an answer she jumped up and down. "You have to go back down to the arena – it's been a whitewash!" she cried. "There's only about eight left to jump and you're going to be placed but you have to hurry! You need to stay on Secret for the lap of honour!"

"W-what?" Alice was confused. She'd jumped clear, but she'd missed out the big scoring joker fence. She'd fully expected to drop down the placings with every round that was jumped after her. As if reading her thoughts, Holly made a mock exasperated face.

"No one has done as well as you. Hurry up!" she chided. "Come *on!*"

Glancing at Finn, who grinned and nodded at her, Alice gathered up her reins.

"Sorry, boy," she said to Secret, who danced a bit from side to side. "Just one job left to do!"

When they reached the arena the fifth to last rider was jumping.

"I totally thought my score would get beaten," Alice said to Holly, who grinned.

"Nope," she said. *"You're* the one to beat!"

"How did you do?" Alice asked her friend. She felt like she and Finn had been up with the horses for hours and hours. Due to the events of the morning and not much sleep, Alice had totally lost track of time!

Holly pulled a face. "Four down," she said cheerfully. "It was super hard! I'm so proud of Minstrel, though. Look, this rider has had another pole down!"

Alice watched the rider shake her head as a pole clattered behind her. Cantering a wide circle, the rider slowed her pony and left the arena to a short burst of applause.

"Jean-Louise Allard, riding Oliver," the commentator said. "Unlucky there, Jean-Louise. Miss Alice Smalley from the United Kingdom is still the one to beat!"

And that's when it started to feel real. Alice held her breath as the next boy jumped, and then another girl. Neither did well or attempted the joker. Alice was still lying in first with one rider, a French girl, left to jump. Alice couldn't believe it!

"This is it!" Holly squealed as the girl rode into the arena. "Alice, I think you might do it!"

But Alice watched as the girl coolly cantered a circle on the most beautiful grey. There was something about her that stood out, her calm manner as she aimed her pony at the first fence, the way she folded so gracefully as her pony seemed to turn a corner in the air, flying on to the next fence and the next, fast but with perfect precision, each fence clear.

The whole arena was silent as the girl and her pony headed towards the joker fence. And, as she cantered past, Alice noticed she had blue stirrups, the ones Alice had always coveted.

It's a sign, she thought just as the pony took off, clearing the joker by miles. The girl flung her arms round her pony's neck as the arena burst into thunderous applause.

And it had been such an amazing round that Alice clapped as hard as she could, knowing that the girl and her pony had thoroughly deserved their win. She knew Secret would be capable of that, and soon. She believed in them. But part of her still felt like crying. She'd wanted to help Finn, and now she couldn't.

"Well, look at that!" the commentator cried. "The top score will stay in France this year. Well done, Eva Ducard and her wonderful pony Swallow!"

"Alice!" Holly was hugging Secret and reaching

up to hug Alice. "You were second, out of *fifty*! And the highest-placed UK rider, that's amazing!"

"You *are* amazing." It was Finn and his voice was overflowing with pride. And suddenly Alice was surrounded by all the pony clubbers, and June and Mathis, and before she knew it she was in the arena for the prize-giving.

"Well done!" she said to the winner.

The girl smiled. "I didn't think I'd beat you. You are the ones to watch!"

And then the flower sash was placed round Secret's neck for winning the highest-placed UK rider, and Alice was presented with the biggest, sparkliest rosette she'd ever seen. And as she cantered around the arena to the crashing, soaring sound of a marching band and the audience's applause, for just a second Alice got a sense of what her future might hold, and it felt incredible.

★
★
★

Chapter 19

"So, now it's my turn to ask – what's up with you?" Finn turned to her as she led Secret back up to the yard, the sash still round his neck, walking contently by Alice's side.

"What do you mean?" Alice shook her head, not quite meeting his eyes. "Nothing's up! I couldn't be happier."

Finn gave her a sceptical look. "Alice, I *know* you,"

he said gently. "You're not secretly disappointed you didn't win, are you? You practically *did*…"

"It would have been nice … the prize money…" Alice blurted out.

Finn frowned. "What?" he said. "You're not seriously upset over that, are you? I mean, I know you love those blue stirrups, but I didn't think you'd feel that upset about not having them!"

Alice stopped Secret and looked right at Finn. "I wanted to help you." She took a deep breath. "I overheard you on the first night talking to your dad about needing money, a thousand pounds, quickly. And what with the Flying Fillies and everything, when I found out what the prize amount was, I thought it might help … so you didn't have to give up." She blushed. "I'm sorry, I should have told you and just been honest instead of trying to make you talk. I didn't mean to interfere."

"That's probably the nicest thing anyone's ever thought to do for me," Finn said quietly. "But I'm glad you didn't risk it."

"But, Finn," Alice continued miserably, "what now? What about the Fillies?"

Finn gave a small smile. "Alice, that thousand we needed was only the start of it, just the first payment." He paused as if struggling with what he was about to say. "We owe a *lot* more than that," he said in a quiet voice. "We're trying to work out what we do as a family, and I thought if I gave up the Fillies then it'd be one less stress for everyone."

He sounded so resigned and sad, despite his smile.

"So that's the end of the Flying Fillies?" Alice felt her heart sink and Finn looked away.

"I don't know, in all honesty," he said truthfully. "This week has been amazing, working with the Rebel Riders. I don't know where I'll go from here."

And then, taking her hand, he pulled Alice closer.

"There was something I wanted to do, up on that hillside." And Alice's stomach turned over as his dark eyes looked right at her and for a few long seconds they hovered, unsure what to do.

But this time it was Secret rubbing his head on Alice's back that pushed her right towards Finn and into his arms. And with the festival in full swing around them and music and laughter in the air, they finally kissed and it was just the two of them, and nothing else mattered.

★

Alice's eyes were full of stars, her heart still beating loudly as she tended to Secret. He had practically swaggered back into the yard, full of his success, the flower sash now minus one or two blooms from where he'd nibbled it. Still smiling, Alice was just hanging her tack back up when Gabby appeared in the doorway.

★

211 ★
★

"Hi, Alice," Gabby smiled. "I hear you did brilliantly! Well done, you and Secret!" Then she hesitated, biting her lip. "Thank you for this morning. I'm still trying to process it all. I knew Maria disliked me; I just never realised *how* much."

"Why did she do it? Was it just to try to get you fired?" Alice felt like a hundred years had passed since she'd caught Maria out that morning. What a night and day it had been!

"Yes, I'm afraid so," Gabby said and sighed. "She tried to mess up the shoots, delete files, that sort of thing. She even cut the reins on the horse's bridle on the first day!"

I knew it! Alice thought. She couldn't believe anyone – especially a grown-up – would behave in such a way!

"And when her subtle sabotage didn't work she took the ring," Gabby continued. "It was just really unlucky that Finn's disappearance coincided with

it all. I don't think she meant it to go as far as it did; she had always meant to 'find' the ring, taking the praise for bringing it back after I'd left the safe open. But then Finn disappeared and we called the police, and suddenly it was all a big mess."

"What an awful thing to do," Alice said, and Gabby nodded sadly.

"Yes. We had a heart-to-heart and she confessed it all. Everything she did was to make me look incompetent. If I couldn't carry off this shoot, it'd prove her point. I've also found out she sent lots of emails to the team back home saying I wasn't up to the job and listing what went wrong."

"Why did she plant the ring in Secret's stable?" Alice asked.

"I think because his is the first stable you come to in the yard," Gabby said thoughtfully. "And he's friendly. She thought she'd found a safe place to stash the ring, somewhere totally unconnected to her. We were all frantic, you see, and everyone was turning out their bags and pockets, and Maria could too, confident in the knowledge that the ring was in the stable yard. But then with all the drama, and Finn being accused and you being here, she couldn't get back to retrieve it."

Alice thought about the hours she had spent in Secret's stable the previous night. She remembered seeing Maria when she was searching for Finn, and the dark look she had given Alice.

"We won't press charges. There's no point," Gabby continued sadly. "Maria has lost her job, and I doubt she'll get another in the same field. So that's that I guess. Everything has consequences." Then she smiled. "What a good friend you are, sticking up for Finn the way you did," she said, and Alice blushed.

"I always knew he was innocent," she said, and Gabby patted her arm.

"Come with me," she said mysteriously. "I've got something to show you."

★

At first Alice wasn't sure what she was supposed to be looking at as Gabby switched her laptop on and started flicking through the photos. Then, peering closer, she gasped.

"Hang on!" she said, a smile spreading across her face. "That's Secret!"

And there he was, trotting across the screen, his red knees lifted high, his mane and tail streaming behind him, the lavender framing his body. Alice couldn't work out when it was taken. Then she realised it was when he'd escaped! Of course, the photo didn't show Alice chasing after him, or an enraged Maria screeching her head off, or the damaged equipment. The photos were incredible – the colours so vivid and Secret so handsome that Alice couldn't stop gazing at them.

"Wonderful, aren't they?" Gabby smiled, and Alice nodded.

"Magic," she whispered. "Just magic."

Then Gabby flicked on through the photos, and Alice moved closer as the screen showed galloping horses with riders throwing themselves off the saddles or standing on broad backs, girls with long wild hair riding side-saddle and Celia and Domino bowing towards each other. And there, Alice felt her heart stop, was Finn, unaware his photo was being taken, dark hair ruffled, patting his horse.

Gabby chuckled. "Our photographer has become a bit of a horse fan," she said. "Not surprising, with these beautiful subjects. We'd like to use the photo of Secret, if we can? It's the perfect natural shot, and we'd pay you well for using it…"

Alice blinked at her. "Wow. And yes please!" Alice imagined opening the glossy magazine and

seeing Secret in there. Of course, one of her main ambitions was to get into *Horse & Hound* with Secret but this would be pretty amazing as well!

"Despite Maria's moaning, the team back in England love what we've done so far, especially your inspired stable-jobs shoot!" smiled Gabby. "The Rebel Riders are coming over to tour the UK and I've put some ideas together for how we can use them. Celia has agreed, which is amazing, and I'm hoping to get Finn on board too. It's only the start of course, but I'm already looking at locations." She made a face. "What I *really* want is somewhere with meadows and a big old house. Somewhere truly unique."

Alice's mind was whirring, and she hurriedly pulled out her mobile phone, now dried out and working, and opened the photo album. There were loads of pictures: her riding Secret last summer in the meadows at Rookham Manor, Finn leading the Dales ponies across the yard, Sasha practising tricks in front of the house. The photos didn't do the yard justice, but you could easily see its beauty.

"Gabby," Alice said slowly, "can I please now show *you* something?"

Chapter 20

Alice decided not to tell Finn about her conversation with Gabby. She had been totally entranced by the photos of the yard, marvelling over the roses climbing up the crumbling walls, the broken clock on the archway, the meadows full of wildflowers. Alice had handed over Angus's number, and Gabby had promised to call him. Crossing back over the cobbles to Secret, she felt a little sick, wondering if she'd done the right thing.

"What have you been up to?" Finn asked, bumping into her in the tack room later.

Alice blushed, their kiss still fresh in her mind. "Oh," she said vaguely, "just this and that."

Finn raised an eyebrow and Alice busied herself with sorting out her grooming kit. She hated keeping secrets from Finn but didn't want to jinx anything by letting him know what she'd been talking to Gabby about. It seemed too good to be true for now.

★

Alice was genuinely sad to pack her suitcase and Secret's trunk. She placed her flower sash and rosette on top, smiling every time she looked at it. Alice couldn't have been prouder of her little red gelding and his willing heart. She'd miss the beautiful yard, and the lavender field, and the amazing arena full of brightly painted

showjumps. But after all the drama and excitement she was ready to go home, and she was determined to help Finn face whatever he had to deal with.

There was a flurry of goodbyes and hugs as the pony club members exchanged numbers and promised they'd meet up soon. Gabby had said goodbye earlier, giving them both a hug. Maria had taken the first available flight home.

Then Celia came to hug her and Finn goodbye.

"We'll see you again soon," she said. "Good things are going to happen for you both. I know it."

Mathis came to wave them off as the ponies were loaded back on to their lorries. Seb appeared by his dad's side on his crutches, and just for a moment he and Alice stared at each other, before Seb grinned and gave Alice a hug.

"Good luck with Secret. He's pretty cool, I guess!" he said, and Alice smiled.

"Thanks. Good luck getting a sponsor."

Then she took Finn's hand and they boarded the minibus, and watched as the chateau and the lavender blurred into a speck in the distance and they were homeward bound.

"Right, Porridge is doing the open ridden on Saturday at Courtley Show, and then Merlin is doing a novice on Sunday at Pine Tree Farm. We'll take Hero and Dolly as well. Then Archie…"

Josephine was consulting the diary, talking at a million miles an hour as she planned the week. Alice hid a smile. They'd barely been back from France for three days, but the summer show season was in full swing and Josephine wanted to get the qualifying classes out of the way. Although she'd scaled down the showing commitments, allowing for Alice's showjumping, they still had a busy few weeks. Secret was out in the paddock having a

well-earned rest, and then Alice would resume her training with Angus.

Alice rescuing Seb was the hot gossip of the pony club branch, with Holly and Sam giving increasingly wild and exaggerated versions of the story, and Alice had what felt like a thousand text messages to reply to from everyone, including Amy, Jordan, Lola and even Hannah. Her success in the showjumping had also been a huge deal, and her mum had actually cried when Alice showed her the flower sash and the photo she'd bought of them leaping one of the bigger fences.

But for Alice the bit she was keeping to herself was the ride out on the hillside, on her beloved pony, Finn by her side, and their kiss after the showjumping. She had relived the moment so many times in her head. She hadn't heard much from Finn since being home, so when he rang her mobile as she mucked out one morning she practically dived on it.

"Hey!" she said a little breathlessly, and she could almost hear Finn smile.

"Hey, yourself," he replied. "So Gabby rang, and Dad and her have arranged a deal. Alice, it's genius! And I know you had *everything* to do with it!"

Alice's heart leapt. Her plan had worked. She just hoped it was enough for Finn to continue with the Flying Fillies.

"Secret needs to make a habit of escaping," Finn said with a chuckle. "It always leads to the best things. Actually, can you bring Secret over for a ride? I … I've missed you both."

And Alice grinned, a blush rising, even though no one could see her.

★

The next day, Alice's mum came out of the office just as Alice loaded Secret, ready to head over to

Finn's house. They were also taking Archie, so Finn could get back to his training with the little Fell.

"Oh, Al," her mum said, "this came for you." She handed Alice an envelope with a pony club logo. *It must be something about the areas, or maybe the trip*, Alice thought, stuffing it into her pocket.

Everyone was in high spirits when Josephine's horsebox pulled up to Rookham Manor.

"Hi, Josie, hi, Alice, great to see you! Wow, it's been a whirlwind these past few days!" Angus looked the most cheerful Alice had ever seen as her mum smiled back. It was like a weight had been lifted from his shoulders. As they unloaded the ponies and led them to the yard he fell into step beside them with Sasha and Finn.

"Gabby, the lady the kids met in France," he explained for Josephine's benefit, "has already been out to see us. She loved it here. We've got a shoot date set for the end of the summer! Alice, we can't thank you enough."

Sasha smiled. "We really can't. You've saved the yard!"

"That's fantastic." Alice's mum put an arm round a blushing Alice. "What quick thinking, I'm so proud of you!"

The fee for using the yard for a week would pay the outstanding tax bill and then some, and there was talk of Rookham Manor being used as a regular location for shoots and even films. Angus explained how they were going to sign up with an agent who would take care of bookings, and the yard could properly start to pay for itself. And Alice, as Secret's owner, was getting paid for her photo, so she would be able to get the blue stirrups after all. It had worked out perfectly!

"I don't know why we never thought about it before," Finn said, as they climbed the meadow a

bit later. The yard was just visible at the bottom of the hill, and they paused, the air completely silent apart from the birds and the occasional pony snort. "It's great, and we don't even need to do *anything*. They love the yard just as it is."

"So you can carry on with the Fillies?" Alice asked, and Finn nodded, but there was the slightest hesitation.

"Yes," he said. "And we'll see where it takes me. I made a promise to Mum I'd carry on stunt riding, and I will."

Alice smiled, imagining a younger Finn and his mum riding together in the very same meadows. And now Finn and her were here together, a stunt rider and a showjumper, riding side by side, united by their love of ponies.

As she stretched her long legs Alice felt something dig into her and she remembered the letter she'd stuffed into her pocket.

227

"Hang on a minute, Finn." She stopped Secret and ripped open the envelope, studying the official-looking cream letter inside.

Dear Miss Smalley, the letter read. *It is with pleasure that we invite you and your pony, Redgrove Secret, to compete at the south of England end-of-summer qualifiers. The winner of the pony club class will be eligible to compete at the Olympia Horse Show…*

Alice had to read it another three times to fully understand it. She read on, the words swimming in front of her.

A colleague closely involved with the organisation was in France for the Festival of the Horse and, as the highest-placed UK rider, your name was put forward.

"What is it?" Finn said in a curious voice.

"A qualifier for Olympia," Alice said slowly, before she clapped a hand to her mouth, turning to Finn with sparkling eyes. "It's for a pony club competition. I'm being invited to try out with

Secret! Me! And Secret!"

"Oh, Alice!" Finn exclaimed. "That's amazing! When's the qualifier?"

Alice quickly checked the letter. "End of August," she said. This was it, this was what she was going to aim for. She wanted that Olympia spot for her and Secret more than anything else in the world.

As if reading her thoughts, Secret turned towards her, nibbling at her boots, his bright eyes affectionate. Alice chuckled, reaching down to hug him, to thank him. He'd helped her achieve things she'd never dreamed possible – and now a new door was opening. Who knew where it would lead them but, whatever happened, Alice knew they'd be together – riding forward into the future.

Acknowledgements

Thank you to the wonderful team at Nosy Crow, in particular Kirsty and Fiona for all their expert help and guidance and Nic for her amazing design skills and for producing the most beautiful covers. A huge thank you as always to my lovely editor Sarah, who totally 'got' Finn and Alice from the start and has been amazing to work with. And thanks to the whole team at Nosy Crow who support the books so brilliantly from start to finish!

Special thanks to Jolie Darton, former owner of Butler – our beautiful cover star. Jolie made sure Butler looked like a superstar ready for his photo shoot! Good luck in your new home Butler!

Finally, writing pony books really is the best job in the world and I must thank my husband Clive who supports me every step of the way despite his own very busy job running the family farm. And of course my children Lara and Jasper, who keep me smiling. I wonder if baby Jasper will follow in the family's equestrian footsteps and become as pony mad as his big sister, whose love for ponies mirrors my own.

If you enjoyed this book, look out
for the Palomino Pony series.

Here's a peek at the first book
in the series…

the
PALOMINO
☆PONY
COMES
HOME

OLIVIA TUFFIN

PROLOGUE

"Just move, Lily. Go forward!" The rider's steely-blue eyes flashed angrily as she sat astride the golden palomino pony. She turned back to her mobile, but not before she had given the little mare a hefty kick.

The pony's nostrils flared and she snorted, but still she refused to walk on. Tentatively, she eyed the bushes ahead of her, her ears twitching back and forth.

"ENOUGH!" the girl cried. "Just do as I say!" With a loud thwack, she brought her riding crop down hard on the pony's hindquarters.

CRACK!

The mare wheeled round with a cry of pain that seemed to echo through the depths of the surrounding countryside. Then, just at that moment, a pheasant exploded out in front of them, squawking and flapping. Catching her footing on the hard, frozen tarmac the startled pony slipped, her hooves scrabbling and sparking.

"I said, go on!" the girl cried out. She struck the pony hard on her flanks again, frightening her even more. The mare reared in a moment of blind panic, tossing her head and showing the whites of her eyes.

The girl was thrown off clear into the road, rolling out of the way as the pony slipped on to her side, scrambling and struggling on the muddy ground.

"Jemma … Jemma … are you all right?" A voice crackled through the mobile lying on the road.

As the girl lay winded and bruised, the pony scrabbled to her feet, her saddle slipping to one side and her reins broken.

Desperate to get away from the girl, the pony wheeled round and galloped wildly down the quiet road, veering on to a track that opened out to the moor beyond. With nothing to stop her, the pony raced and raced as if her life depended on it.

When she had covered at least three miles, the palomino finally slowed. She snorted into the clear crisp air, her breath hanging in a silver plume. She was safe at last.

CHAPTER ONE

"Phew, what a day that was!" Georgia slumped into her seat as the dark-green horse lorry pulled out of the showground. It was the first time she'd had a chance to relax all day, she'd been so busy grooming, plaiting and polishing. She hadn't actually ridden herself but she wasn't complaining. She loved being around horses and it was a real treat watching them compete.

Georgia especially loved Wilson, the big bay thoroughbred cross, and there was no doubt about it – he'd definitely been the star of the show! Georgia smiled as she pulled her tangled golden hair back into a ponytail. Wilson was owned by the Haydens – Sophie and her mother, Melanie – and was just one of the ponies that Georgia helped looked after in their yard.

"Thanks again for everything you've done today, Georgia," said Melanie as she drove the horse lorry down the bumpy old track and joined a long queue of horseboxes making their way home. "We couldn't have done it without you, could we, Sophs?" She turned to her daughter.

"Er, what was that?" Sophie looked up from the text she'd been busily composing.

"I said we couldn't have managed without Georgia's help today, could we?" Melanie frowned at her daughter, who was still engrossed in her phone.

"Er, no," Sophie mumbled. She was sitting between her mother and Georgia, a handful of rosettes spread across her lap.

Sophie sounded uninterested but Georgia knew that she wasn't being offhand. She just wasn't passionate about the looking-after part of being around horses, in the way that Georgia was. Sophie was going off to university next year, and at the moment her friends and her social life were probably more important to her than winning at the show.